5/05

EVERYTHING WRIGHT

EVERYTHING WRIGHT

●

Katrina Thomas

AVALON BOOKS
NEW YORK

PRINTED IN THE UNITED STATES OF AMERICA
ON ACID-FREE PAPER
BY HADDON CRAFTSMEN, BLOOMSBURG, PENNSYLVANIA

For Doug, my favorite hero.

Chapter One

"**I**'m going to get married, and you can't stop me!"

Meghan Blake's younger sister's words echoed against the thick walls of her office as she forced herself not to react with undo shock. Sarah's tendency to over dramatize situations may have helped her develop skills as a drama student, but became an annoyance when she was attempting to relay accurate information.

Meghan turned her attention to the file in her hand. "I want a complete update on the buyout negotiations with Taylor Enterprises, Carly."

The executive assistant entered notes on a laptop computer balanced on the edge of Meghan's father's functional metal desk as she glanced at Sarah, who had turned her back to them and was staring out of the row of plate glass windows overlooking the James River. "I could come back later, Miss Blake."

Before Meghan had a chance to respond, Sarah swung around to face her older sister. "No, don't go, Carly. That won't be necessary. My future happiness has got to be less important than the business of running Blake Industries."

"Sarah." Meghan kept her voice calm and quiet and without emotion. "That will be all for now, Carly, and tell my secretary to hold my calls for the next five minutes."

"Of course, Miss Blake. You have a meeting with the vice president of Blake Publishing at eight-thirty. Should I have your secretary reschedule it?"

Meghan shook her head. "Just give us a few minutes."

The door closed behind her executive assistant without a sound, and Meghan folded her arms in front of her. "Now, what is all this about, Sarah?"

Her sister's hazel eyes seemed to stare a hole through Meghan's head. She tossed her auburn hair over one shoulder and dropped into a chair next to the desk. "Zach and I have decided to get married. See?"

She held her left hand out to Meghan. On her ring finger was a thin band of white gold adorned with a single diamond chip. "We're engaged."

Meghan took a few moments to study the ring as anxious thoughts filled her mind. Marriage was such a serious commitment, such a frightening prospect. How could her little sister be contemplating such an important step in her life?

"Is this serious?"

"Serious?" Sarah's hazel eyes widened. "Of course, it's serious. Didn't you hear me, Meghan? Zach and I are getting married. In the lives of most people, that is a serious decision."

"Who is this Zach?"

Sarah blew out a puff of air. "Zach Dunn, my boyfriend for the past year. He spent spring break with me at the beach house. He's my best friend. I talk about him all the time. Don't you ever pay attention to anything except work?"

Meghan picked up a pen from her desk and rolled it between her thumb and forefinger. "And you and Zach have discussed this matter?"

"It's not a matter. It's a wonderful, happy development in our relationship—and yes, we've been discussing it almost daily for months now."

"Marriage is a very serious step."

"We know. It means commitment to each other and, someday, to a family."

"Having children will be expensive."

Sarah narrowed her eyes as her jaw tightened. "Having children is a wonderful experience that people who are in love share. Just because you despise the idea of marriage and hate children doesn't mean everyone else in the whole world feels the same."

"I don't hate children."

"I think you've always hated me ever since I was a baby. You've punished me all my life for being born five years after you and for having a mother who didn't die before I had a chance to get to know her."

Her sister's words stung her, but Meghan tried to remain calm. "That's not true, Sarah. I care about what happens to you. What does Zach's family think about your plans?"

"We haven't told them yet." Sarah flipped another strand of auburn hair over her shoulder. "Zach wanted to tell you first. He wanted to come with me this morning, but I told him that it would be better if I came alone. With your schedule the way it is, I wasn't sure you'd even take time to see me. We're meeting his uncle for dinner this evening."

"Sarah, you know that I will always see you. You don't need an appointment."

"You never have time for me. You're constantly working."

In an attempt to avoid another argument, Meghan sighed. "Zach's uncle lives in Virginia?"

Sarah shook her head. "No, Zach's whole family is from the Boston area, but his uncle, Zach's guardian, is here on business."

"What kind of business?"

Sarah threw up her hands. "Only you could care more about the way the members of Zach's family make their livings than his love for me, or his views about raising children or his commitment to family."

Meghan dropped her pen on the desk and smoothed the black-lined fabric of her fitted jacket. "Certainly, I would like to discuss your marriage plans further with both you and Zach, but I'm afraid I have no spare time today or tomorrow. Perhaps this weekend at the beach house, when we celebrate Grandma's birthday and the Fourth of July—"

Sarah rose to her feet. "Oh, just forget it. Don't bother to fit us in. Zach and I will manage without you. Anyway, I doubt if you'll be able to pull yourself away from all of this to spend even part of the weekend with anyone not connected to Blake Industries."

"Sarah—"

The sound of the office door slamming behind Sarah as she rushed from the room echoed in Meghan's ears. For a moment, she stared at the empty space where Sarah had been standing, and then lowered herself into her desk chair and covered her face with her hands.

Her head pounded with tension. Her mind was reeling from the news of her younger sister's wedding plans. She hated arguing with Sarah. That was all they ever did, it seemed. Unsolicited tears burned her cheeks.

A knock on the door caused her to brush her face dry with her hands. Her secretary's blonde head appeared in the doorway. "The representatives from Blake Publishing are waiting for you in the conference room."

Meghan inhaled a deep breath. "Distribute copies of the projected profits report and tell Carly we're ready to begin." She rose from her chair. "I'll be right there."

"Of course, Miss Blake. I'm afraid your sister ran out so

quickly that I couldn't catch her in time. She left her purse in the reception area."

Meghan nodded. "Just put it in a safe place. I'm sure she'll be back for it when she realizes she's forgotten it." Sarah was so irresponsible. She thought she was ready for marriage, but she could not even keep track of her purse!

Later that afternoon, Meghan was working on her computer when her secretary knocked. Rubbing her tired eyes, she expected an announcement that Sarah had returned for her belongings and had decided not to go through with the preposterous notion of getting married.

"Geoffrey Wright is here to see you. He doesn't have an appointment. Will you meet with him, or should I set up a more appropriate time for you?"

Meghan stared at her secretary. "Geoffrey Wright? He's here? Now?"

"He's waiting in the reception area. Will you see him?"

She took a steady breath. The president of the Wright Company had finally decided to face her in person. Without the obligatory telephone tag between secretaries and initial meetings between lower ranking representatives, he had simply arrived—making an unexpected appearance to her office on one of her worse days ever, no less.

Was he attempting to impress on her the fact that he controlled the situation? Was it so important to him to choose the time and place of their meeting?

She picked up a pen and rolled it between her fingertips. It was up to her now. She could still take charge and make him wait. Causing the great Geoffrey Wright to bide his time while she cleared her schedule for him would probably teach him a lesson in humility, but she had been anticipating this moment for over a year. She did not think she had the forbearance to wait any longer.

She nodded to her secretary, who was standing patiently in the doorway. "Tell Carly to begin the four o'clock board meeting without me, and show Mr. Wright in." She rose to her feet. "Has my sister returned yet?"

"No. I've tried to reach her several times."

"I'm sure both her phone and pager are in her purse. I'll see if I can find her as soon as I finish speaking with Mr. Wright."

With the palms of her hand, she smoothed the front of her dark jacket and set a warm welcoming smile on her face as she waited to meet her visitor. Despite her mental preparation for his actual arrival, Meghan had difficulty suppressing the sudden excitement she experienced at the thought of meeting the man in person once again.

Geoffrey Wright could not help but exude power and wealth. For a moment, she allowed herself the luxury of assessing the incredibly handsome man before her. He stood over six feet tall, dressed in a dark, expensive Italian suit and a silk shirt. His short, dark brown hair, gray eyes the color of the ocean before a summer storm, the slight hollow of his cheek bones, and a strong determined chin combined on a face that was breathtakingly attractive in her eyes.

With reluctance, she pulled her attention back to the reason for his presence in her office and held out her hand. "Mr. Wright, how very nice of you to take time out of your busy schedule to meet with me."

As he leveled his eyes on her and shook her hand, she noticed that his smile, although warm, was edged with hesitancy and caution. Why had he come? Why had Geoffrey Wright, the president of the Wright Company of Massachusetts, traveled all the way from Boston to Newport News to see her? The resolve in his expression warned her that the conversation he planned to have with her would not necessarily be pleasurable or without obstacles.

Realizing that she was still holding his hand, Meghan

pulled from his grasp and reached for a pen on her desk in an unsuccessful attempt to steady her shaking fingers. "Please, sit down."

She hoped that her voice projected the self assurance she was far from feeling at the moment. Why was she so nervous? Her confidence did not usually fail her in business or in social situations. What was wrong today? She watched him settle his tall frame in a chair in front of her desk and admired the way the fabric of his suit formed over his broad shoulders and long legs like a second skin.

"I apologize for arriving unannounced, Miss Blake. I appreciate your seeing me on such short notice."

She took a seat behind her desk and crossed her legs as she tried to focus her concentration on the fact that the head of one of the most prosperous and influential medical supply companies in the United States was in her office. "Please, it's Meghan. Am I correct in assuming that this is a business call?"

He smiled and revealed a set of perfect, white teeth. "Actually I was in the area on a personal matter and realized that the headquarters of Blake Industries was just minutes away from my hotel. I took the chance of seeing you without an appointment. I understand that Blake, under your guidance, has taken a special interest in a small firm my father began several years ago as a subsidiary of the Wright Company."

"Yes, Wright Pharmaceuticals." Meghan nodded as she attempted, with some difficulty, to curb the excitement created by the thought of a possible purchase of the Wright family's company. Her nerves were taut with anticipation of verbal volleying that led to the financial transactions and business mergers that were a significant part of her life. She met his eyes with equal challenge. "Under your leadership of the past eight years, the Wright Company has grown into a notable competitor in the medical technologies field."

He raised dark eyebrows above his gray eyes. "I can take very little credit for our success. Having had the opportunity to be guided by the past diligence and fortitude of my deceased relatives, I lead many dedicated and exceptional employees who work much harder than I do to achieve our company's goals."

She smiled at the sincerity of his humble admission. "I have been a casual observer of the developing status of several small medical research firms, including your own Wright Pharmaceuticals."

His eyes narrowed. "As far as I have been able to surmise, your interest in my firm has been much more than casual."

"Blake Industries has been monitoring a number of similar companies all across the country, Mr. Wright." She rolled her chair forward and folded her hands on her desk blotter. "We have not singled out Wright Pharmaceuticals."

"Please call me Geoffrey, Meghan." His words sounded friendly, but she watched a shadow cross his handsome face. "Your representatives have been actively investigating my family's firm. Your familiarity with the specific details of our research data and current marketing strategies makes me suspect that your curiosity is much more ambitious than you are willing to admit."

She cleared her throat as waves of excited anticipation rippled in her stomach. "Mr. Wright—Geoffrey—Blake Industries is prepared to offer you a substantial settlement for the sale of Wright Pharmaceuticals. I think that you will be interested in our vision of future growth for this small, yet valuable, division of your family's company."

She watched his jaw tighten as he said, "Wright Pharmaceuticals is not for sale."

Prepared for, and challenged by, his opposition, she squared her shoulders. "I'm sure you'll find our offer more than generous. Please, listen to what we have to say."

"I'm afraid that it would be a waste of time for both of us, Meghan. Money is not an issue here."

She smiled. "Money, Geoffrey, is always the issue."

"Your assertiveness and persistence are quite impressive. It is obvious that you have done nothing but improve your business savvy since your undergraduate days at Harvard."

Meghan fought to keep a blush from rising up her cheeks. "You remember? I assumed that our brief meeting nine years ago had completely slipped your mind."

"You were a lovely, energetic young woman eager to learn everything possible about the business world, in which, I understand, your father had immersed you since you were just a child. As I recall, I could not respond to your onslaught of questions quickly enough."

She nodded. "And you were a reluctant but highly effective teacher, Geoffrey. Your detailed description of the establishment and growth of Wright Pharmaceuticals has continued to inspire me as an outstanding model for the creation of a thriving small business."

"Your boundless enthusiasm and interest in commercial enterprises amazes me. I suppose it is an achievement of sorts to have played a small role in inspiring such a prominent leader in the business world. I accept your compliment." He rose from his seat. "With that, I shall take my leave and waste no more of your time. Good afternoon, Meghan."

Disappointed but far from defeated, she stood and rounded the corner of her desk. Offering her hand, she forced a smile. "I don't think we are finished, Geoffrey, but I am late for a meeting now. Perhaps we might get together again before your return to Boston. How long will you be staying in Newport News?"

When he took her hand, she nearly jumped as an electric jolt seemed to pass from him to her fingertips and up her arm. The excitement of doing business with Geoffrey Wright had been dampened because she had lost the first battle. Why, then, did she feel such agitation stirring within her?

"I doubt that we have anything left to discuss. Wright Pharmaceuticals is not for sale."

She hid her frustration with dignity. "Appealing to your sense of fairness, I am asking for a second chance. Meet me again, and hear my plans. If you absolutely abhor my ideas, I promise to rescind my offer to buy your firm; and we never have to see each other again."

His dark gray eyes bore a hole into her soul as he studied her in silence. With a sigh, he finally nodded. "Very well. I would be remiss if I were to deny that I am immensely irritated by your persistence, but I admire your determination."

"Does this mean you'll meet with me?"

"At the moment, I cannot make a definite appointment to meet with you again because I have a pressing personal matter that requires my attention—but I'll leave my hotel number with your secretary."

Meghan watched him stride from her office and disappear down the corridor to the elevator. She attributed the sudden sense of disappointment she experienced to the fact that she had been unsuccessful in convincing him to sell his family's small medical research firm. Pushing thoughts of dark gray eyes and broad shoulders in Italian fabric to the back of her mind, she gathered file folders, computer, and briefcase and hurried to the conference room.

That evening, Meghan sat at her desk again and studied reports from the board meeting, as well as notes her assistant had taken. The office building was quiet and empty. Few employees stayed after dark during the summer months— most of them rushed home to spend time with their families and friends. Meghan alone stayed late, working far into the night. The sky was clear and filled with stars. She could see the lights of the Newport News shipyards and the waterfront restaurants and small specialty shops. In the privacy of the still office, she sighed. The day had been long and full of business and personal challenges.

Where was Sarah? She had not returned to the office, and Meghan was worried. Had she been too critical of her sister's plan to marry? Was this marriage idea more than just a passing fancy to Sarah? Tolerance for Sarah's fickleness was not one of Meghan's strong traits, she knew. How did Zach Dunn fit into this mess? Was he as indecisive as Sarah, who had changed her major three times since the beginning of her freshman year at Harvard? Was he any more responsible than her sister?

As concern for Sarah weighed on her mind, Meghan was also plagued by the lingering distraction of her brief meeting with Geoffrey Wright. He was a business opponent, a challenge to her skills of creative persuasion. She was confident that she would someday convince him that selling Wright Pharmaceuticals was in his company's best interest, but confused by the fact that she had not been able to sweep his handsome, intriguing features from her mind.

He had changed very little since that colloquium nine years ago, when he had been one of the guest speakers presenting to interested freshmen. The dark gray eyes and determined chin came to her mind at the most inopportune times and threatened her unshakable ability to concentrate under the most difficult of circumstances.

A soft knock on the open door interrupted Meghan's mental wanderings, and she looked up to find Sarah standing there with red eyes and a tear stained face. Her heart melted as relief flooded over her. She rose as her sister ran into her open arms.

She held Sarah as the young girl sniffled. "I know it's a

hard lesson to learn, but it's for the best. You're just not ready for a serious commitment like marriage."

Her sister pulled away from her and glared. "You sound just like Zach's uncle!" Her hazel eyes flashed with anger. "What makes you two old, domineering, terribly responsible individuals think you know what's best for us?"

Old? At twenty-six, Meghan did not consider herself old, but she realized that in her sister's young, restless, and immature mind she probably seemed ancient. Rather than being insulted by Sarah's accusation, Meghan accepted it as a fact of life.

"So Zach's uncle was less than enthusiastic about your wedding plans too?"

Tears streamed down Sarah's face, and Meghan wrapped her arms around her sister once again as she cried into her shoulder. "He hated the idea."

Curbing her expression of relief that a faceless stranger shared her view of the prospective union, Meghan handed Sarah a box of tissues from her desk. "He doesn't approve then?"

With her pale face wet with tears, Sarah shook her head. "We don't need his approval, and we don't need yours either. Zach and I are still getting married, whether you like it or not."

Meghan swallowed her anger as her newfound hope was dashed in an instant. "Listen, Sarah. Let's just sit down and talk this over calmly." She urged her sister into her chair and leaned against the edge of her desk.

She waited until Sarah wiped her face with a tissue and then turned red rimmed eyes up to her. "Why do you have to get married? What is the rush? Why don't the two of you take some time to date and get to know each other better? Marriage is such a permanent step."

Sarah chewed her bottom lip for a moment, and Meghan was reminded of the same gesture her grandmother used to

make before she began to say something she considered pro-
found. Her sister's shoulders squared. "I wouldn't expect a
pessimist like you to believe in true love or fairy tales
because you've never read anything but the *Wall Street
Journal*; but, I want to live happily ever after with my Prince
Charming, and I don't want to wait." She leaned toward
Meghan. "I believe that Zach and I have the real thing. We're
in love."

"You're twenty-one years old, Sarah. How can you know
what love is?"

"Age has nothing to do with it. Being older hasn't made
you wiser on the subject of human relationships. You might
be more open to our getting married if you went out on a
date once in awhile." She threw a wadded tissue at her. "An
emotionally starved cynic like yourself would probably end
up talking about business the whole evening, or spend the
night sharing financial reports."

Unwilling to admit to the accuracy of her sister's words,
Meghan tossed the tissue over the edge of the desk into the
nearby wastebasket. "My social life is none of your concern.
We were discussing you."

Meghan's mother had died when she was an infant. So
Meghan had been raised by her father, John Blake, a professed realist with little tolerance for frivolous idealism and
romantic notions. Meghan had never allowed herself the
luxury of useless imaginings or flights of fancy regarding
what her life would be like with someone to love or someone to return that love. Sarah had had, for a few years, the
influence of a mother, John's third wife, who had taught the
child silly ideas of hope and love and romance.

For a moment, a picture of Geoffrey Wright flashed
through Meghan's mind. A slight flutter danced in the pit of
her stomach as she imagined him meeting her at the door
when she arrived home after a long day at the office.

She shook her head. Imagining his comforting arms embracing her was completely ridiculous. It was such a waste of time. Why had she thought of him? They were business adversaries. That was all. Confused by the direction her thoughts had taken her, Meghan pulled herself back to her sister. "Where is this devoted fiancé of yours? Shouldn't you be comforting each other at a time like this?"

The questions were out before she realized how cruel and uncaring they sounded. She watched more tears spill from Sarah's eyes.

Handing her the box of tissues, Meghan rubbed the younger woman's trembling shoulders. "I'm sorry. I shouldn't have said that. My distrust of any human relationship not involving a contract does not give me the right to judge yours."

Sarah blew her nose and grinned. "We decided together that he should stay with his uncle at the hotel tonight. Zach really cares about what his uncle thinks and hopes he can persuade the old guy to accept our wedding plans."

" 'Old guy,' Sarah? You should be more respectful of older individuals. How would you like Zach to call Grandma an old woman?"

Sarah shrugged slender shoulders. "Well, I suppose, he's not that old, not as old as Grandma, anyway; but he acts old and thinks like an old man. He's so serious and inflexible, just like you."

"I'm not inflexible, just cautious, especially about your happiness. Sarah, I just want what's best for you."

Sarah hugged her. "I know you do, but I'm not one of your companies. You can't just dictate to me anymore and expect me to comply. While you were busy with corporate mergers and negotiations, I grew up."

Meghan inhaled a long steady breath. She wished she could be more confident about her little sister's ability to make wise decisions concerning her future.

"Tell me again how you and Zach met."

"Are you sure? You already admitted you can't even remember who he is."

"I remember; thin, cute, intelligent, friendly, but a little shy."

"That's him, except he's more than cute. He's devastatingly handsome."

"I don't remember the devastating part."

Sarah grinned and clasped her hands together in front of her chest. "We met at a business colloquium for prospective business majors."

Meghan did not hide her surprise. "You're a business major?"

"I was, for a few weeks. Anyway, I went for the free *hors d'oeuvres*, and that's where I met Zach."

"Then he is a business major?"

"No, he doesn't like anything to do with finance and marketing and industry, but his uncle was one of the presenters that evening. Zach just went to give a little moral support."

Meghan tried not to let her temper flare at the lack of commitment both Sarah and Zach had toward their future careers. "You attended a reception on a program you despise for the free food?"

"Sure, why not? You know I don't like Harvard. I wanted to go to New York City and take acting classes, but you insisted. I was miserable there until I met Zach."

Her sister's words filled her with guilt. After becoming Sarah's legal guardian when their father died, Meghan had struggled to make the right decisions concerning her capricious sister's future. It had been with good intentions that she had pushed Sarah into attending school in Massachusetts. Most people did not make a decent living being an actor. She had hoped Sarah would learn to accept that fact and appreciate the value of a good education.

"I have Grandma to thank for that."

"For what?"

"For talking me into trying business as a major. She said she had not wanted to interfere with your authority as my guardian, but she knew it was really important to you that I show a little interest, at least, in Blake Industries."

"Grandma said that?"

"Yes, in one of her lucid moments before she got so bad. At her suggestion, I took a couple of classes. I still hated business, but I ended up going to the business colloquium and meeting Zach."

Sarah's voice bubbled with enthusiasm for her fiancé, and it did not escape Meghan's notice. Was it possible that she was completely wrong in assuming that this marriage was such a bad idea? Could it be that Sarah and Zach truly loved each other? Did she dare let her little sister take that risk, even if it meant that Sarah could end up with a broken heart? Meghan's stomach muscles tugged with concern.

"We didn't even like each other at first. I thought he was too quiet. He thought I was too bubbly. But he liked the way I always cut my pizza before I eat it, and I liked his smile. For awhile, we just met on campus and walked around and talked. Last Christmas, he invited me to his family's home on Cape Cod, remember?"

"Yes. I remember, but I guess I didn't realize that your relationship with him was anything more than a brief infatuation."

Sarah shook her head. "We were strolling on the beach with the blustery December wind blowing when Zach told me he loved me. I'd been in love with him for months. We were so happy. At Easter on a warm beach in Waves, he proposed and gave me this ring."

"You've been engaged for over two months?"

"We were waiting for the right moment to tell you, but there never seemed to be a perfect time." She shrugged. "We didn't want to wait forever."

Meghan forced herself to remain calm. "Does he have a job, Sarah?"

Her sister grasped her hands and squeezed. "Zach loves me. He cares about what I think. He likes the way I eat pizza with a fork."

"How do you and Zach plan to pay for these pizzas you eat with a fork?"

Sarah's hazel eyes sparkled, and Meghan held her breath. "Zach's an artist, a photographer. He's going to be famous someday."

Meghan chose her words with care. "What do you plan to live on until he gets his big break in the art world?"

"Oh, we're not worried about food and a place to live. We're going to take a year or two off from college and help some poor, starving people in South America."

Chapter Two

The image of her protected, inexperienced sister living in a rugged mountain village or near a jungle crawling with poisonous insects, without the financial support to which Sarah was accustomed, would have caused Meghan to laugh if she had not been so shocked. She doubted that Sarah's professed love for Zach Dunn, and his for her, could sustain the young couple through cold nights and hungry days—not to mention the months of inclement weather, or the probability of political unrest and even guerilla attacks. Shuddering at the thoughts that raced through her mind, Meghan swallowed a command forbidding her sister to be so reckless. This marriage to Zach was a terrible mistake, but she would have to come up with another approach if she was going to convince Sarah of that fact.

"Look, Sarah, I don't know about all of this. How much thought have you and Zach actually given to these plans of yours? Please don't rush into anything, especially something so dangerous and unfamiliar."

"We're not rushing. Anyway, it's not up to you. There once

was a time when I would have done anything to please you. I wanted to relieve the loneliness and isolation I felt after my mother died. What I wanted from you—what I thought I needed from you—was your attention and approval and love; but I don't need any of those things anymore. I have Zach now."

Meghan watched Sarah as she turned to leave. "We're still family."

Sarah shook her head. "No, not really. I see what Zach's family is like. They talk with each other. They listen. They care. They spend time together. That's what family is—the way it used to be before my mother left, before Grandma got sick, and before you decided that work was more important than us."

Guilt stabbed in the pit of Meghan's stomach. Her sister was right. She knew that, but she was not sure how to improve their relationship. Had she let the fragile bond between them deteriorate to a point that was beyond repair?

"I don't suppose you're coming home soon."

Meghan glanced at her desk. "I have a lot of work to do."

"Suit yourself. Maybe Grandma will still be up. I can share my good news with her. She might not understand, but she'll listen without criticism."

As Sarah opened the door leading to the office building corridor and elevators, she stopped and turned to Meghan again. "As long as they're here in Virginia, I invited Zach and his uncle to the beach house for the weekend. Zach wants his uncle and me to spend more time getting to know each other, and Zach wants us to try to spend some time with you. I warned him not to get his hopes up, but I thought inviting his uncle for a Fourth of July celebration on the Outer Banks couldn't hurt any of us."

"I'll be there, Sarah. I promise. Tell Zach I look forward to meeting his uncle and getting to know both of them.

Don't forget about Grandma's birthday on Saturday. I've
arranged a small party for her."

"Don't *you* forget."

The elevator closed on her sister and the stillness of the
air in the deserted office building hung around Meghan like
a heavy fog. She returned to her desk and, exhausted, fell
into her chair. She was tempted to run after Sarah and go
home with her. *Why am I staying? Nothing on my desk is so
urgent that I can't do it tomorrow.* Before the thoughts
formed in her mind, she knew the answer. She glanced
around the large, empty office that seemed more like home
to her than the family house she shared with Sarah and her
paternal grandmother. She would spend the night there
working just as her father had done so many nights, long
ago, when Meghan had been growing up. Tormented by
failed marriages and unhappy personal relationships, John
Blake had often chosen to remain in the secure—if not
entirely comfortable—setting of the headquarters of Blake
Industries. Her father had removed himself from the whole
complexity of family and feelings by retreating to his office,
which had been complete with a bathroom, a small sleeping
area and a closet holding several changes of clothing.

Meghan's gaze drifted to one of several bronze sculptures
by her father's favorite artist. Frederic Remington—a writer,
sculptor and painter who had captured in his works the spirit
and sense of adventure of cowboys and Native Americans on
the western plains—had always inspired John Blake.

She recalled many evenings resting her elbows on the
edge of her father's desk as she studied these bronze images
and listened to her father describing his dream of moving
west, of buying a horse ranch, and of embarking on solitary
journeys into the untamed wilderness. With impatience, she
brushed stray tears from her eyes. John Blake had never

achieved that dream. He had died of a heart attack just after Meghan graduated from college.

He had taught her that working hard and being successful in the financial world was the only fulfilling endeavor in one's life; but now she wondered if he truly believed in that philosophy when he himself had longed for a different life, one of freedom and exhilaration, of wide open plains and few responsibilities. Had he wanted to escape the stress and demands of running a business, or was his dream of moving west just another way to avoid his failed personal relationships?

She shook her head as she pushed the power button on her computer. The more she tried to figure out John Blake, the more confused she became. Her father had taught her about business, and she now possessed the confidence and skills needed to make decisions that ultimately affected herself, her family and thousands of employees who worked for Blake Industries. On the other hand, she felt completely unprepared for the situation she now faced concerning Sarah. Her father had suffered three unhappy marriages before he died. What would *he* have done about Sarah's plan to dive into such potential pain and sadness?

Geoffrey skimmed through the water with strong, rhythmic strokes. The scent of chlorine filled his head like a drug every time he pushed his face above the surface and inhaled a long deep breath. Exercising in the warm water should have relaxed his taut muscles. In the past, swimming laps had always helped relieve tension from his body; but, of course, today had been anything but usual.

After fifty laps in the deserted hotel pool, he was just as irritated as when he had begun. The vigorous exercise did not seem to help him forget the events of the past day, even though he tried with diligence to ease the uncomfortable feeling he was experiencing. Breathless, he stopped to clutch the tiled edge of the pool and attempted to calm his racing mind.

Zachary's announcement that he planned to marry Sarah Blake had come as a surprise to him, although he had noticed over the past few months that his young nephew was becoming increasingly infatuated with the smiling, cheerful woman with auburn hair and hazel eyes—who seemed more interested in the campus drama club than in declaring a major or getting passing grades in her classes. If Zachary was more decisive about his own career choice, his fiancée's lack of planning would not seem so significant; but as Zachary's legal guardian, Geoffrey could not help worrying about their determination to make such an important lifetime commitment with only their love for each other to sustain them.

On a more disturbing note, Geoffrey continued to berate himself for not realizing until a few weeks ago that Zach's Sarah was none other than the younger sister of Meghan Blake, the president of Blake Industries, the former Harvard freshman who had intrigued him over nine years ago with her endless string of questions and inquiring deep brown eyes. Was she behind this whole marriage idea?

John Blake, her father, had had an infamous reputation in the business world for being both highly successful and incredibly shrewd. Geoffrey's father, also an effective businessman, had held John Blake in high esteem and had often mentioned his admiration of Blake Industries' remarkable ascent to become one of the top privately owned companies in North America. After meeting with Meghan earlier that day, Geoffrey had no doubts that she had inherited the skills John had possessed, and that she continued to expand and to develop her father's company since his death five years ago.

Could she have manipulated a situation in which his

nephew would meet her sister, to contrive a connection between the Wright Company and Blake Industries that would create initial dialogue, at least, involving the potential sale of the firm Geoffrey's father and uncle established? Aware of the fact that Meghan was respected by business allies and adversaries alike, he could not help but wonder if that respect had been earned, or if it had been the result of coercive and underhanded practices. Would the young woman stoop so low as to use her own sister to get what she wanted?

For years after their first encounter at the business meeting, the image of Meghan Blake—with her bright oval face, high cheek bones and thick lashes edging huge brown eyes—had, at odd times, entered his thoughts. After seeing her earlier that day, he could not get her out of his mind. She was a constant distraction. Why? He was not even sure he liked her very much. He certainly did not understand why he found her so alluring after nine long years.

"Hey, Geoff. Here you are."

In surprise, he dragged his thoughts back to the present as he focused his eyes on his nephew entering the pool area through a glass door. The younger man squatted down near the edge of the water.

"I've been looking all over for you, Uncle. Don't you usually do your workout earlier in the day? It's past midnight."

"I needed to do a few extra laps." Geoffrey pulled himself out of the pool and reached for a towel. "What's up?"

"Grandma called. I was on the phone with Sarah, so the front desk took a message from her. Apparently she's been trying to reach you on your cell phone. Don't you have it with you?"

Geoffrey rubbed his short hair. "I refuse to be 'on call' every minute of the day."

Zach grinned, and Geoffrey was reminded of the small,

wiry, eight-year-old boy left orphaned when Geoffrey's older sister and brother-in-law died in an automobile accident. His nephew had changed very little in appearance since Geoffrey had become his guardian thirteen years ago.

"That's what Sarah says. She thinks telephones and pagers and computers are a real intrusion on human relationships. She says her family relies too much on technology and hardly ever shares in genuine, effective communication."

"Intrusion is a very good word for such annoyances. On that particular point, your fiancée and I seem to agree. What did your grandmother want?"

"She left an urgent message that she needed to speak with you."

"Urgent?" Geoffrey's heart quickened. Amanda Wright was a self-reliant, independent woman, who never called to engage in trivial conversation. She had been traveling abroad for most of the past year, making infrequent calls to her only son; and when she did, she always had a reason. "Did she leave a number where she can be reached?" He was already heading toward the door.

"I'm sure everything's fine. She's somewhere off the coast of Greece with Joe and Phoebe Dalton on their yacht, and she asked the desk to tell you that she'd call back to your room in half an hour. It's early in the morning there. She's probably just getting ready to have breakfast."

Geoffrey had time enough to rush to his room and shower before the telephone rang. Slipping into a robe, he hurried to pick up the receiver. "Mother, hello. What's wrong?"

"Nothing is wrong, Geoff. It's wonderful to hear your voice. I'm having a marvelous time on our cruise of the Mediterranean. I'm calling because I heard that congratulations are in order."

"Congratulations?" He sank down on the bed as relief flooded over him.

"There's going to be a wedding, I hear."

"Yes, your grandson is determined to marry Sarah Blake. News is certainly traveling fast these days."

"Zach and Sarah!" He could hear the surprise in his mother's voice. "Not you, dear? I must have gotten the message wrong."

Geoffrey chuckled. "You thought I was the one planning the wedding?"

His mother sighed into the telephone. "I had hoped for another grandchild or two before I'm too old to enjoy them."

"I'm afraid you're going to have to settle for great-grandchildren, Mother."

"So, you haven't found the woman of your dreams, my dear?"

"No." He pushed a mental picture of Meghan Blake from his mind. The president of Blake Industries was definitely *not* the woman of his dreams.

"Are you looking?"

"No, not really, Mother. I'd rather not get into this whole discussion tonight."

"Very well, Geoff, but I worry about you being alone so much."

"I'm not alone. Zach's staying here at the hotel in Newport News with me."

"You know very well that that's not what I meant, but I'll respect your wishes for the moment. Do you have business meetings in Virginia this week?"

"No, I was in Baltimore at a sales conference earlier this week, and then I flew down here to see Zach. Tomorrow, he and I are driving out to Hatteras Island to spend the weekend at Sarah's family's beach house."

"What a nice treat for you. Sarah's a lovely young woman. She and Zach are very much in love."

"You knew?

"Of course."

"I think they're both too young."

"Now, my dear, try not to be overly protective. Our Zach is old enough to make his own decisions. We have to trust that he will make responsible choices."

"He and Sarah want to quit college and go help people in some underdeveloped country."

"And when you were their age, you were spending every free minute you had at the local youth center helping under-privileged children."

"We're not talking about me." Geoffrey felt his grip on the receiver tighten, but Amanda's laugh warmed his heart. He could never stay angry at his mother for very long. "We miss you, Mother. When will you be home again?"

"I miss you too, darling. I'll be back at the end of the month, and then we'll have a big family party at the house on Cape Cod. Give Zach and Sarah my love. I have a marvelous engagement gift in mind for them."

Geoffrey tossed and turned all night. Whenever he managed to doze off, his restless sleep was interrupted by reruns of his conversation with Meghan Blake. As dawn inched its way into his room Friday morning, his thoughts left him feeling exhausted and irritable.

The thin, oval face with high cheek bones and a determined chin were imprinted on his mind. Edged with thick curly lashes, her chocolate eyes glistened with excitement as she strove to convince him that her offer to buy his family's pharmaceutical firm was so enticing that he would find the proposal irresistible. Strands of dark brown hair, held back from her face by a barrette at her nape, shone in the sunlight reflecting off the water outside her office window. Her long, slender neck, adorned with a single string of lustrous pearls, exuded an air of aristocracy that she deserved by being the daughter of John Blake and the president of one of the most prosperous companies in the country.

Rolling over onto his back, he listened for sounds of movement from the other bedroom in the hotel suite he shared with Zach—but only silence and the throbbing of a tension headache drummed in his ears. Realizing that his nephew must still be sleeping, Geoffrey threw the blankets from him and swung his long legs over the side of the bed.

As he dragged a hand through his sleep-tossed hair, he heaved a sigh of relief that he had not mentioned to his mother his suspicions regarding Meghan Blake's role in executing the future union of her business to his family's. Hoping to be wrong, he did not want to concern Amanda without necessity. If he was right, she would learn of the deception soon enough. What concerned him even more than his mother's reaction to the truth was the great pain Zach would experience if he discovered that Sarah was involved in such betrayal.

He paced back and forth across the floor. For everyone's sake, he had to find the truth. He had to know what role, if any, Meghan Blake had played in his nephew's initial meeting with her sister and in the events leading up to the subsequent engagement. Conniving to create an artificial relationship between the Wright Company and Blake Industries was despicable, and gambling with the emotions of two young college students was even more contemptible. If Meghan, with or without Sarah's help, had been in any way responsible for plotting to deceive his beloved nephew, Geoffrey would not stop until he exposed the scheme and forced Zach to accept the truth.

On an impulse, he picked up the telephone and punched in the number of Meghan's office at Blake Industries. He had to see her as soon as possible. Although he realized that the hour was early and that it was unlikely the offices were even open, he thought that perhaps he could leave a message with her answering service that he needed to see her before the weekend.

Even though he would have preferred to meet her unannounced to catch her off guard, he dared not take his chances visiting her without first notifying her office. She could quite possibly refuse to see him until she decided on the time and place.

As the telephone rang, he prepared a brief, yet firm, statement to recite into the receiver; but when the ringing was interrupted, the voice he heard was neither recorded, nor did it belong to an answering service employee.

"Blake Industries. Meghan Blake speaking."

"Meghan? It's Geoffrey Wright. Good morning." He stumbled over the words as her confident feminine voice echoed in his ear.

"Geoffrey, what a pleasant surprise. What may I do for you?"

"Well, I was hoping to get a chance to see you, briefly, this morning.'

"I'm sorry, but my day is completely booked up."

He had to admit that she was good at feigning indifference. If she were anxious to discuss a deal to purchase Wright Pharmaceuticals, she certainly hid her feelings well. "Are you sure you can't possibly squeeze me in? I had hoped to see you before I left."

"Oh, you're leaving?"

Was she really going to continue the charade of pretending to be unaware of the holiday family party at her own beach house? He tried to detect a note of deception in her voice, but he heard none. "Only for the weekend. We're going to spend some time at the beach."

"Perhaps we could meet when you return or—"

Geoffrey felt a glimmer of hope. "Or?"

"I'm free right now, until my first appointment at seven."

"You start your appointments at seven in the morning?" Geoffrey made no attempt to hide his surprise.

She laughed, and the sound calmed his raw nerves despite his continued suspicions of her. "When I can. I'm an early riser—and I have some personal matters to attend to later today, so I wanted to leave the office early. Can you come here to my office, or would you prefer another meeting place?"

"Your office is fine. I'll be there in twenty minutes."

She met him at the front entrance of the building. He noticed that the street was deserted. Meghan flashed him a bright, welcoming smile as she disengaged the security system before holding the glass door open for him.

Although it was just 6:30, she appeared as if she had been awake for hours. As Geoffrey followed her into the elevator, he gave the young president of Blake Industries a visual perusal. She wore white pants with wide legs and a black fitted jacket with gold buttons. Standing just inches from her, he realized how petite this powerful businesswoman actually was. Even in high black leather pumps, she barely reached his shoulder. The faint scent of her floral cologne seemed to fill the whole elevator and reminded him of a New England meadow on a summer afternoon.

As the door opened, she led him through the reception area and into her office. "The receptionists don't begin work until seven." Leading him to a corner filled with blue upholstered chairs and a low, polished, dark walnut table, she gave him another smile. "Please have a seat, Geoffrey. I ordered coffee and rolls from a nearby deli in case you hadn't had breakfast yet." She settled into one of the chairs across from him. "Now, what may I do for you?"

He searched her deep brown eyes for a sign of deceit, a clue of her intentions—but he could read nothing in her expression. He knew he needed to discover the truth, but he had not yet planned out his strategy for obtaining it.

She offered him a cup of coffee and waited with her hands folded in her lap. As she sat with poise and confidence and quiet patience, Geoffrey felt completely unprepared. Why had he not taken the time to plan his strategy?

With no better idea in his mind, he thought of the one issue that would seize her attention. "I've been considering your interest in Wright Pharmaceuticals."

She raised dark, sculpted eyebrows above liquid eyes. "You've changed your mind?"

He gave her a hesitant smile. "Let's just say I haven't completely rejected the idea."

She unfolded her hands and leaned toward him across the low table. "And what have you been considering?"

"Well, it's not only my decision to make, of course. My mother will have to approve any transaction between our two companies. She is vacationing abroad right now."

"I understand. I'll be happy to meet with your mother when she returns from her trip."

He set his coffee cup on the table in front of him. "Why are you bothering with such a small, insignificant company? You have Blake Medical, Blake Research, Blake Pharmacology and even Blake Healthcare. Why such interest in Wright Pharmaceuticals?"

"It hasn't turned a profit in five years."

"The research firm has always been solvent."

Meghan sat back in her chair and nodded. "Solvent, yes— but is it as successful as it could be?"

He allowed himself a few moments to recall what he knew about the company his father and uncle has initially established as Wright Pharmaceuticals. Now both deceased, the two brothers had had high aspirations for the small drug company and had invested a lot of money into its marketing and drug production—and even more into the research and development department.

He remembered that Zachary, his uncle and his father, Peter, had actually enjoyed playing an active role in the daily operations of the small division of the Wright Company, despite its lack of significant financial growth. As the current president of the family business, Geoffrey realized, with some nagging guilt, that he had given the pharmaceutical firm very little attention since the deaths of his father and his uncle.

Meghan refilled his cup with coffee from a thermal carafe. "Do you honestly believe Wright Pharmaceuticals has reached its ultimate potential in the thirty years of its existence? I want to make that happen, Geoffrey. I believe Blake Industries can assist your company to thrive and improve its present productivity." Her large brown eyes held his in a steady gaze. "I don't want to destroy what your father and uncle created. I want to help it prosper and grow."

With reluctance, he pulled his eyes away from her bewitching look. The idea that she could probably talk him into anything with those alluring eyes scared him. She had so much drive and enthusiasm for business. Despite his suspicions of her, he found himself considering the challenge it would be for the man who decided to tear down that wall of emotional and psychological control she preserved with such prowess.

It was obvious to him that he would not discover the truth of her motives today. With a heavy sign, he rose to his feet. "I'll notify my mother of your offer, Meghan. Thank you again for seeing me on such short notice."

As he held out his hand, he tried to read in her eyes a hint of her intentions beyond the seemingly genuine concern she expressed, but he could see nothing. What he felt, though, as she shook his hand was altogether different. As their fingers touched, he experienced an intense burst of electrical sensations that pulsed through every nerve in his body and, in an instant, left him agitated and breathless. Never in his life had he had such an acute reaction from shaking another's hand.

Had Meghan felt it, too? Her eyes revealed only a smile; and with a quick, awkward movement, he pulled his hand from her warm, gentle grasp.

"You'll contact me after you have spoken with your mother?"

"Yes, yes, of course. She may want to set up a meeting. Although she doesn't play an active role in daily family business matters, she likes to be kept informed of major decisions."

She looked at him with bright friendly eyes, and her smile widened. "I look forward to hearing from both of you, Geoffrey. Have a nice weekend at the beach. Will you be going up to Virginia Beach or down to the Outer Banks?"

Was she serious? Was it possible she did not know about his relationship to Zach? He cleared his throat. "We're going to spend time with friends on Hatteras Island."

"Oh, that's a beautiful place. The weather is supposed to be perfect, although I've heard that a tropical storm has been forming in the Atlantic."

He almost blurted out the questions that had eaten away in his mind all night long. *Why don't you just admit that you concocted this whole elaborate scheme? Why don't you just come clean with the entire plan so we can all go home? You wouldn't have to carry this charade any farther, especially throughout the whole weekend, and waste any more of our time. Just say it, Meghan Blake. Admit you used your sister and my nephew to get Wright Pharmaceuticals.*

The words formed in his thoughts but never reached his tongue. Instead, he returned her smile, nodded and left her office.

Meghan watched as Geoffrey Wright's tall figure disappeared behind the closing doors of the elevator. Staring down the empty corridor, she rubbed the palm of her right hand against the fabric of her pants leg.

The throbbing sensation that had vibrated up her arm and throughout her entire body as she shook his hand continued to pulsate even after he had gone. Confused and unsettled, she gave her palm another vigorous rub before returning to her office, where his fresh scent of soap lingered everywhere.

Why had he come? What had been so urgent that he needed to meet with her that morning? The discussion had been the same as yesterday, as far as she could tell. What purpose had today's early meeting served?

With a sigh, she began to pile file folders together and slide them into the large worn leather briefcase her father had used whenever he attended meetings outside the office building. Despite her bewilderment regarding Geoffrey Wright's behavior and her unexplained reaction to him, she acknowledged her growing respect for his strong loyalty to his family's business. When she had begun the pursuit of Wright Pharmaceuticals, she had assumed that he cared little for the small medical research firm. In planning her strategy to match her determination, she recognized that she had underestimated his own resolve. The acquisition process would not be as simple as she had calculated.

Chapter Three

"**S**he's absolutely right. It's breathtaking here."

"Who's right?"

Geoffrey watched Zach as the younger man kept his eyes on the North Carolina State Route that ran the length of the narrow band of land off the eastern coast. He had not realized that he had spoken his thoughts aloud.

"Oh, nothing." He turned his attention to the spikes of marsh grass on Pea Island National Wildlife Refuge bending in the hot summer breeze on the right side of the road. On the left, the sand dunes, covered with waving sea oats, rose high enough to obscure a clear view of the ocean surf.

"You're awfully quiet today, Zach."

"I'm kind of tired, I guess. I didn't sleep well last night."

"Your bed wasn't comfortable?"

His nephew chuckled. "No, the accommodations were exceptional, as always."

"There are few such accommodations in underdeveloped countries."

Zach shot him an irritated look before returning his eyes to the road. "I know that."

"Does Sarah?"

"Is that what this is all about, Geoff? You think that we are two naive, spoiled college students who don't know about the hardships of life outside of our own small, protected world? Give us a little more credit than that."

"I don't know Sarah well enough to make that judgment."

"It's not your job to make judgments at all."

"That's exactly what your grandmother told me." He watched a grin brighten Zach's somber face.

"Oh, she did, did she? So, she finally reached you. Is everything okay?"

Geoffrey's eyes followed a flock of seagulls swooping around the sand dunes they were passing. "Yes, she wanted to congratulate me on the announcement of my wedding engagement."

"Your engagement? What an incredible idea!"

"Exactly. She's very disappointed it wasn't mine, but she's delighted about you and Sarah. She sends her love."

Zach nodded. "We planned to call her this weekend. Rochelle Dalton must have mentioned it to her parents who told Grandma. I wonder how the news got so mixed up that she thought you were getting married."

"Probably her own wishful thinking." Geoffrey's tone was dry. "She wants more grandchildren."

"You can hardly blame her, Uncle. What are you now, thirty-five? Are you going to let that bit of bad luck you had all these years ago stop you from finding true happiness?"

"I believe that true happiness comes from within oneself—and that bit of bad luck, as you call it, was a huge blow to my ego, not to mention my confidence in mankind, especially the female type."

"Just because your fiancée eloped with your best man two days before your wedding doesn't mean you have to be cynical about all women. Open your heart again, Geoff, and give someone else a chance."

"I think you should mind your own business."

Zach chuckled again. "And I think you should mind yours. Let Sarah and me make our own decisions. You have to trust us."

"I trust you, Zach, but that's not the point. What do you know about Sarah Blake, anyway?"

"I know that I love her."

Geoffrey resisted the urge to give his young nephew a lecture on the concept of love. Such a speech would hardly ring true, as it had been a long time, if ever, since he had experienced any feeling that remotely resembled romantic love. He stared at the calm expanse of the glistening water of Pamlico Sound that separated Hatteras Island from the North Carolina mainland. If he had been in a better frame of mind, the scene of endless sea and sky would certainly have left him in awe. Now, he just pulled his gaze back to Zach.

"I just want to know why? Explain to me why this marriage to Sarah is so important right now. You have your whole life ahead of you, Zach."

"I love her, Geoff."

"But marriage is such an important step. Maybe you should take some time to think about it."

The chill inside the sporty rental car had nothing to do with the air conditioning unit. For several moments of intense silence, Geoffrey watched Zach, whose mouth tightened into a thin, white line and whose hands gripped the steering wheel with added force. "We have, Uncle. We've thought about it and talked about it and discussed it and now we want to get married. We want to share our lives together. We want to start a family of our own."

Zach sighed. "You've been a wonderful parent to me, Geoff. After my parents died, you were generous and caring in your concern for my upbringing. I wouldn't have made it without you and Grandma. Don't you see? Sarah and I want the opportunity to give that kind of love and security to our own children. You act as though falling in love is a crime."

It is if someone manipulated the circumstances to produce a false relationship. The words echoed in his mind, but he did not speak. For the rest of the trip, both he and Zach remained silent.

Geoffrey did not dare speak for fear that he would say something he would later regret. With relief, he gazed out the window as some large, wooden buildings came into view. As they approached what appeared to be a village, he noticed that most of the unpainted structures were elevated several feet above the ground by wooden supports, and were decorated with elaborate porches, balconies and decks of all sizes and shapes.

"This is Rodanthe, the northernmost of the seven villages on Hatteras Island." Zach reduced his speed. "The Blake family beach house is located in Waves, the next town. Salvo, Waves and Rodanthe make up a quiet, little tourist community here on the upper part of the island. The three used to be all one town called Chicamaconico, but they separated in the early twentieth century. There are miles of unoccupied land and beaches on both the sound and ocean sides beyond Salvo and before Avon, the next village."

Zachary made a left turn and drove along a straight narrow street. "The Blake house is on the north edge of this cul-de-sac ahead of us. Across the wooden walkway over the dunes is their own stretch of long, quiet beach and surf. It looks like it's going to be a beautiful day."

"Who else is coming?" Geoffrey's thoughts drifted to the meeting he had had with Meghan earlier that morning. Would she be coming too?

"Sarah says that for weekends like this, when the whole family and other guests are planning to stay at the beach,

some of the household staff are sent down early from the
Blake estate on Chesapeake Bay to prepare the house. The
cook and a maid arrived last night, and Sarah, her grandmother and her grandmother's nurse will be here for lunch."

"That's all? No one else is coming?"

Zach pulled the rental car into a parking space between
sturdy supports holding the large beach house several stories
above them. "We invited friends who are arriving tomorrow,
and, of course, Sarah's sister will be here, but her schedule
is very unpredictable. Many times, business matters come
up at the last minute and keep her from joining in planned
family events. Sarah's always getting upset at all of the time
Meghan spends working." He glanced at his watch. "If we
grab our bags and take them up to our rooms, we'll have
time to go to the beach before lunch."

Geoffrey rounded the car and lifted his garment bag and
matching leather suitcase from the trunk. A hot, damp
breeze warmed his skin, and the refreshing scent of sea air
raised his spirits. He hoped that the weekend of relaxation
would help improve the circumstances that had begun to
strain the relationship he shared with his nephew.

An hour later, Zach chased Geoffrey across the white
sand and flopped down onto the blanket they had brought
from the Blake beach house just a few hundred feet behind
them. After swatting his uncle with the edge of his towel, he
used it to wipe his water drenched hair. "Before the weekend's over, I promise I'm going to give you a good dunking.
I must have swallowed a gallon of salt water and sand when
you caught me by surprise and pushed me under."

"Thanks for the warning. I'll keep my guard up."
Geoffrey chuckled as he wiped his arms and shoulders. "I'm
amazed at the warmth of the water."

"Isn't it gorgeous? When I came here with Sarah at

Easter—it wasn't as warm as it is now, of course—but we could still go swimming. At our beach on Cape Cod, the ocean sometimes doesn't even get warm enough for me in July. The beaches are so different here. There's white sand for as far as you can see and no jutting rocks to break up the endless, awesome landscape."

Geoffrey looked out over the huge expanse of ocean and allowed himself to be mesmerized by the rhythm of the powerful surf. Waves formed and approached the beach and then leveled out before retreating, just to return again. The unrelenting ebb and flow of the water had always had a relaxing effect on him. Today was no exception, although the sense of foreboding that had been nagging at him ever since Zach and Sarah had announced their wedding plans continued to hover in the back of his mind.

"We should probably get back to the house." Zach rose to his feet. "Sarah should be here now."

Geoffrey draped his towel around his shoulders and stood up. As Zach folded the canvas beach chairs, Geoffrey shook sand from the blanket. "How long have you and Sarah known each other now? It's been over a year, hasn't it?"

His nephew shot him a warning look. "It was a year ago this past spring. We met at that business colloquium for prospective business students. You did your usual presentation on the Wright Company, remember?"

Folding the blanket into a manageable size to carry back to the house, Geoffrey nodded. "That was the first time you ever saw her?"

"Yes, although we may have passed each other on campus before that evening. I can't say for sure." Turning, Zach gave his attention to the tall, slender figure hurrying toward them. "Here comes Sarah now."

Geoffrey watched the young couple embrace in an obvious expression of affection. It was apparent as he observed them that Sarah and Zach thought what they felt for each other was love, but he could not be sure that it was the true kind of love that would sustain them through all of the hardships and heartbreaks of life.

"How was your trip down, sweetheart?" Zach draped an arm around Sarah's shoulders.

"Oh, fine. We didn't have any problems, but it seemed to take forever because we had to stop every thirty minutes so Deanna and I could help Grandma out of the car for a break." She gave Geoffrey a shy smile. "Are you coming back for lunch? We'll be eating soon."

Zach nodded. "Geoff and I were just collecting our beach stuff."

"Good. You'll show your uncle where the showers are, right? I have to get back and help Grandma get settled. My sister won't be coming until later, but everyone else is here until our friends arrive tomorrow."

Zach kissed his fiancée and then waved as she ran toward the Blakes' large beach house rising several stories above the dunes. Geoffrey thought the structure looked more like an elaborate mansion of wood than a seaside vacation home. He thought it would not be hard to get lost in such a place.

"Sarah tried to talk her sister into taking today off from work to start the weekend early and meet you, but I guess Meghan couldn't." Zach adjusted a folded beach chair under each arm. "As far as I've been able to tell, Meghan Blake doesn't do anything but work."

That was, of course, the impression Geoffrey had gotten from his two recent meetings with the young woman; but he did not share his opinion with Zach. Instead, he said, "Does Sarah take an interest in the running of Blake Industries?"

His nephew shook his head as he led the way along the boardwalk. "No, she actually dislikes anything to do with business. She hasn't any interest at all in finances or marketing or the management of personnel. I guess that's always been a big argument between Sarah and her sister. Sarah's kind of apathetic about Blake Industries, but that company is Meghan's whole world."

Zach stopped for a moment to readjust the chairs under his arms. "You'll meet her later. Maybe you'll make a better impression on her than I have. I'm not even sure she knows who I am."

Geoffrey pondered Zach's comment. "I look forward to meeting everyone in Sarah's family."

"You're going to love her grandmother. She's a lot older than Grandma. I guess she didn't have her son, John, until she was in her late forties. In her lucid moments, she shows lots of spunk and can even put Meghan in her place. I'm sure she was quite a character in her time."

"In her time?" They approached the storage shed where the beach equipment was stored, near one corner of the large pool that spread across the back length of the beach house.

Zach glanced around the empty pool area and lowered his voice. "From what Sarah tells me, about three years ago, Hilary Blake, John Blake's mother, began to show some memory loss and disorientation and was soon diagnosed with Alzheimer's disease. I met her only a year ago, but I've definitely noticed her condition getting worse just in the past few months." He shook his head. "Watching their grandmother getting sicker has been hard on both Sarah and Meghan. Sarah's scared about losing another member of her family and afraid she'll lose her sister too, while Meghan retreats further and further into her world at work. Even though Sarah disagrees with me, I think that Meghan is just as afraid as Sarah is about losing her grandmother, but is simply using her responsibilities at Blake Industries to try to forget her fears. They're not a close family like we are, Geoff."

His nephew gave him a boyish grin, and Geoffrey smiled. He watched as Zach set the chairs in the shed and took the beach umbrella from him. "Members of the Blake family don't share everything like we do. They aren't plagued by those meddlesome summer reunions and infamous Christmas celebrations at Cape Cod."

Geoffrey nodded. They were lucky. Although they had lost many people close to them, he and Zach and Amanda still gathered at regular intervals with family and close friends to celebrate holidays, birthdays and special occasions. He hoped that he and his nephew would be able to resolve their present differences without jeopardizing their participation in cherished family traditions.

After meeting Hilary Blake, who was confined to a wheelchair due to the results of a stroke she had suffered several months earlier, and her nurse Deanna Fuller, who, according to Sarah, had been hired by Meghan soon after Hilary had been diagnosed with Alzheimer's disease, everyone sat down and enjoyed lunch. When Deanna excused herself and left with Hilary, Zach and Sarah announced their plans to go to the beach.

Declining the young people's invitation to join them, Geoffrey decided to take a walk. When he returned and found the house devoid of activity, except in the kitchen where the cook was busy making dinner preparations, he swam his usual number of laps in the pool and then read a book on the fourth floor deck, from which he could see both the Atlantic Ocean on the east side and Pamlico Sound on the west side of the island. As his eyes drifted from the words on the page to the white caps dotting the endless expanse of the sea and the clear blue sky above it, he wondered when Meghan Blake would be coming to the beach house. He was anticipating her arrival, but he did not know why. Yes, he wanted to face her and to find out the truth regarding her role, if any, in Zach's engagement to Sarah—but confronting her would not be pleasant. What he was experiencing while he waited for her appearance was restless excitement. What did that mean?

At 8:30, dinner was served to Zach, Sarah, Geoffrey, Hilary and Deanna. Although Zach attempted to lighten his fiancée's mood with teasing and humorous topics of conversation, Geoffrey noted that Sarah was growing increasingly upset as the night progressed. From her frequent comments, he guessed that she was angry because her sister had not yet arrived. He tried to recall Meghan's words at their morning meeting. She had indicated that she planned to finish her work early but, to most people, after dinner was not early.

As the maid began to clear the table, he followed Zach and Sarah upstairs and out onto a large balcony that overlooked the pool area and the moonlit beach beyond it. He watched Sarah pace across the wooden floor.

"Where is she? Meghan promised to be here by dinner."

Zach caught her shoulder to stop her nervous walking. "Maybe she had car trouble or a flat tire along the way."

Sarah shook her head. "She would have called. No, this is typical Meghan behavior. Work is always more important than anything else going on in her life."

She pulled away from Zach and turned to Geoffrey. "I'm sorry my sister's being so rude. Don't take it personally though. Unless you are a business client or associate, she treats everyone with the same indifference."

The tears in the young woman's hazel eyes pulled at his heart. Meghan Blake may be skillful in the business world, but her personal one was falling apart. "Zach's probably right, Sarah. Perhaps you should call her."

"No." She gave her auburn head a firm shake. "It'll just make me angry if she hasn't even left her office yet. We argue too much as it is."

She tossed a strand of hair over her trembling shoulder.

"Would you like something to drink? We have lots of fruit juices and coffee and tea in the kitchen."

Zach reached for her hand. "I'll get drinks for us. You just stay here and relax, sweetheart."

Geoffrey crossed the balcony to lean against the railing as Zach entered the house through the sliding glass doorway, and Sarah resumed her pacing. The moist, warm ocean breeze had a refreshing effect on him despite the fact that he was unable to push thoughts of Meghan's chocolate brown eyes and long thick lashes from his mind. Without conscious effort, he said a silent prayer that she was safe and, as Sarah suspected, simply allowing business to take priority over family obligations. He could not dispel the odd sense of protectiveness he was experiencing toward a young woman he knew neither needed nor desired his help.

He watched Sarah retrace her steps across the balcony once again. "It's a beautiful night."

"Yes." She sighed and stood next to him at the railing. "Hatteras Island is one of my favorite places." She balled her fists at her sides. "It used to be Meghan's favorite place too."

"Has your family had this beach house many years?"

"This one, no. Father had it built the year before he died. Before that, we had a comfortable little cottage in Salvo that belonged to Grandpa and Grandma. We used to come down to swim and fish and stay with them there."

"Do you like fishing, Sarah?"

She raised her eyes to the sky and shrugged her shoulders. "We used to go fishing all the time on Father's boat, *Blake's Bounty*. Father and Meghan landed a marlin once. It was huge."

In the lights strung along the outside perimeter of the balcony, he could see her eyes brighten. "I like surf fishing too, right off the beach. You and Zach should try it while you're here. Maybe we could even talk Meghan into going out on the yacht with us to do some deep sea fishing, if she ever gets here."

"Your sister must have a great deal of responsibility running a company as large as Blake Industries."

Sarah nodded. "Too much, I guess. She never has time for anything else."

"Do you have plans to join her in your family's business?"

She stared at him as her hazel eyes widened. "Me, in business with Meghan? You've got to be kidding. We can't even be in the same room for two minutes without arguing."

"But didn't you and Zach meet at a business colloquium?"

"Yes, remember? That's where I met you, too."

"Zach went because I was making a presentation that night; but if you're not interested in business, then why did you attend?"

She looked at him with a steady gaze of innocence. "At the time I hadn't declared a major, and I went to please Meghan."

"So, your sister knew about your attendance there that evening?"

"I thought she would be happy, but she barely noticed."

"She encouraged you to go then?"

"Meghan never encourages. She bullies and criticizes and tells me what to do."

Geoffrey was frustrated that he could not get a straight answer from the young woman. Was she being purposely evasive? "But she recommended that particular business colloquium?"

Sarah stared at him. "Why so many questions, Geoff? Zach always says that even though you're legally in charge of the Wright Company, you're not obsessed with business and money like my sister is. Why are you so curious about my interest in it all?"

"Curious about what?" Zach's quiet voice interrupted Geoffrey's clandestine quest for the truth. In an instant he felt a sharp pang of guilt stabbing in his stomach.

He watched his nephew cross the balcony and offer Sarah a tall glass of iced tea from the tray in his hands. "What have I missed?"

Sarah sipped her drink. "Your uncle wants to know why I went to that business colloquium where we met."

Zach's eyes narrowed as he handed Geoffrey a glass of tea. "And why is that, Uncle?"

Weighing the odds of damaging his relationship with Zach even more than it had been already, Geoffrey chose his next words with care. "I have reason to suspect that your initial meeting with Sarah was not a coincidence."

"What do you mean? Of course, it was. Zach and I had never even met before that night."

For a moment Geoffrey held Zach's angry eyes over the rim of his glass before meeting Sarah's confused ones. "Didn't you admit that it was your sister's idea to attend the colloquium?"

"Admit? Now you sound like Meghan. I thought we were just talking."

Zach slipped his free arm around Sarah's shoulders. "It sounds like more than that. You don't have to answer any more questions."

"I don't mind, Zach. I don't have anything to hide."

She turned to Geoffrey. "Whatever you think, there wasn't any conspiracy around my meeting Zach the first time. It was actually my grandmother's idea that I go to the colloquium."

"Your grandmother's?" He did not try to hide his surprise.

"Yes, before she had her stroke and before the Alzheimer's disease took so much from her. One day, she happened to see a list I had of upcoming events on campus and suggested that, since I was still trying to figure out what to do with my life, I attend the business colloquium and see if I might have an interest in it."

She looked up at Zach and smiled. "As it happened, the only good parts of the whole evening were the food and meeting Zach. I never mentioned any of it to Meghan until afterwards, when I told her I had definitely decided not to major in business."

His nephew glared at him. "Are you satisfied?" He turned to Sarah. "I think I've heard enough. Come on. Let's go for a walk."

"Wait, Zach, Sarah—" Geoffrey watched the younger man urge the young woman toward the steps that led to the ground floor. "I just wanted to make sure."

Zach stopped at the top of the steps and turned toward him with flashing eyes. "The only thing we're sure of, and the only thing that matters, is that Sarah and I love each other, Uncle. You and her sister can interrogate and suspect and threaten all you like, but nothing is going to change our minds. Sarah and I are getting married whether you like it or not."

Geoffrey watched the couple descend the stairs and disappear into the night. In the distance, the steady rhythmic sound of the surf contrasted with the tumultuous battle of regret and self righteousness raging in his body.

Someday, he hoped Zach would understand why it was so important for him to find out the truth. *Is it worth risking the loss of my nephew's love and trust?* He asked himself that question again and again as he headed toward his bedroom on the third floor of the quiet beach house.

After tossing and turning for the second consecutive

night, he awoke the next morning before sunrise and slid from his bed. Although it was still too dark to see, he could hear the ocean surf as the waves formed and crashed and then slipped back to sea. He tried to figure out how he was going to make things right again between Zach and himself. At the same time, he wanted to dispel the concern for Meghan who, to the best of his knowledge, still had not arrived at the beach house.

Had something happened to her? Had she had an accident? He was not sure why, but he could not push from his mind the image of her stranded along a deserted highway, or hurt and alone somewhere between Newport News, Virginia and Hatteras Island, North Carolina.

He pulled on his swimming trunks and headed for the pool. Maybe his daily exercise routine would help him get his mind off Zach and Meghan. The house was still and quiet when he left his room. As he stepped out onto the deck of the pool, the warm, moist sea air filled his lungs, and he could hear the surf pounding just a few hundred feet away from him.

The surface of the pool water was as smooth as glass, and he sliced it with his body as he took a dive into its clear heated depths. The liquid encased him like a wool blanket in winter and gave him a moment of unconditional comfort. With vigor, he began to cover the length of the large rectangular pool with powerful strokes. For awhile, he allowed the rhythm of his breathing and the warmth of the water to calm his restless mind.

Several minutes later, he heard someone approach and pulled himself to the pool's edge. Hoping that Zach had forgiven him and was coming to talk, Geoffrey took a seat at the far end and dangled his feet in the water.

"Oh, I didn't know anyone was out here."

The sound of her voice shook him, and he imagined that

his mind must be playing tricks. He had thought about Meghan and dreamed about her so often during the past two days that he was now fabricating her image speaking to him.

"I came out to watch the sunrise."

He stared at the petite woman approaching him and realized that the image was real. She was not a dream this time. He inhaled a deep breath of warm, moist air. She looked enchanting in the sunrise. "Good morning, Meghan."

It appeared obvious that she was just as surprised to see him. Her huge brown eyes widened. "Geoffrey? What are you doing here?"

He tried to read veiled deceit on her pale face but he saw only surprise and wonder. He watched her hands flutter at her sides, and he smiled at her. "Your sister invited me. Didn't she tell you?"

Chocolate eyes stared back at him. "You're the *old* uncle?"

He cleared his throat. "Am I to understand that I'm being insulted?"

She shook her head. Her expression was unreadable to him. If she had been expecting him, she certainly hid the knowledge well.

He pushed strands of wet hair back from his face. "Did you just arrive?"

"Yes, I had planned to drive down last evening, but some things came up. I was at my office until after one."

He watched her rub her eyes with her fingertips. "How's the temperature of the water?"

"It's fine. Why don't you join me?"

"No." She gave her head a firm shake. "I don't like the water."

He slid back into the pool. "Are you sure?"

Her hands fluttered at her sides again. "If you'll excuse me, I have to unpack my car. Please, enjoy your swim."

Chapter Four

After Geoffrey had completed his morning laps, showered and dressed in shorts and a T-shirt, he entered the quiet dining room and took a seat at the empty table. As the maid offered him coffee, he wondered where Zach and the members of the Blake family were.

Meghan's reaction to his presence at the pool confused him. Her surprise had appeared genuine. He wanted to trust her and to know that she had not instigated Zach's engagement to her sister. He wanted to believe she would not use Sarah to get to him or to his company. He also could not ignore the relief he felt that she had finally arrived.

Her presence at the beach house delighted him. Why did he care? What was it about Meghan Blake that kept him up at night and invaded his dreams when he slept? Why did it disrupt his stable, logical thinking with regularity and intensity—not only since the previous day, but often throughout the time since their first meeting nine years ago?

The relentless, persistent thoughts of her baffled him. No woman had ever had such a powerful effect on him. Memories of her fascinated him—her eyes with mysterious, enticing depths and her quick, intelligent mind with the constant need to explore every aspect of an issue and to challenge easy, conventional solutions. He knew when he first met her, a bright freshman, that she was unique—a student with unlimited professional potential and unstoppable drive. Now, meeting her again after almost a decade, he could not help wondering if she lived her personal life with such intensity as well.

As he sipped his coffee, he was struck with subtle uncomfortable pangs of envy that gnawed at his stomach for the man fortunate to share Meghan's most intimate thoughts and feelings. Who did she trust? With whom did she confide? Certainly he did not wish to be that chosen person, did he?

The maid set a plate of scrambled eggs and wheat toast on the table in front of him. "Mr. Dunn and Miss Sarah have already left, Mr. Wright. They said they would be having breakfast in Nags Head before going over to Roanoke Island for the morning."

With effort, Geoffrey pulled his thoughts back to less perplexing questions. "Roanoke Island?"

The uniformed maid nodded as she poured him a glass of orange juice. "I believe they mentioned going to the marine aquarium in Manteo, but they plan to be back by noon because they are expecting their friends here for a beach party at one. At Miss Sarah's request, the cook will be serving lunch at two o'clock."

Finding the prospect of eating alone rather bleak, Geoffrey pushed his plate of food away. The fact that Zach and Sarah had not invited him to join them that morning did not surprise him. He deserved their anger and contempt. So far, he had not been very supportive of their decisions or objective. With great effort, he tried to dispel his fears that Sarah was involved in any plan to lure Zach into an insincere personal relationship for the sake of Blake Industries' growth. As he observed her with his nephew, she appeared to care for him; and it was obvious that Zach had deep feelings for her. He would definitely have to work on improving his attitude toward their prospective marriage, or even his own mother would stop talking with him.

Finishing his coffee, Geoffrey rose to his feet. He was supposed to be spending time with Zach and Sarah, but that plan did not seem to be working out as well as he had intended. Well, at least he would get a lot of reading done.

With a sigh, he strode to the arched doorway between the dining room and living room. *I should probably just fly home to Boston. I'm wasting time hanging out at the beach in North Carolina, especially when my reason for being here in the first place has sneaked off to watch fish in a tank all morning.* He was reluctant to leave without first satisfying his suspicions that Sarah and Zach's meeting at that college colloquium was part of Meghan's scheme to obtain possession of Wright Pharmaceuticals. He needed to know the truth, even if that meant risking Zach's scorn and anger.

For a moment, he stopped to admire the plain yet appealing decor of the large, open-beamed living room. The colors were soothing; a collection of creams, light greens, and beiges. The mission style furniture, with its vertical slats of pale oak and light lacquer finish highlighted the whole room. Beyond the chairs and sofas were three sets of glass doors that opened onto a second floor balcony overlooking the ocean. The view was breathtaking.

Geoffrey crossed the marble floor toward the wall of spotless glass before him. If he had not felt so miserable and alone, he would have been able to appreciate the scene before him, but his dark mood prevented him from taking even the slightest bit of pleasure in the awesome sight before him.

He pushed open one panel of glass. While staring at the ebb and flow of ocean waves on the sand, he was startled by a sound to his right. When he shifted his gaze toward the noise, he noticed for the first time that beyond the balcony was a small porch enclosed by screens.

From where he stood, he could see someone leaning over the thin, frail figure of Hilary Blake in her wheelchair. For a moment, he thought the person standing was the elderly woman's nurse, but then he heard the soft feminine voice he recognized unmistakably as Meghan's.

"There, Grandma. Are you comfortable? Let me tuck this blanket around your legs. Is that better? The breeze is a little cool this morning, but it's supposed to get extremely hot today. The weather report said the temperature will reach the mid-nineties."

Geoffrey watched the president of Blake Industries rearrange the cotton wrap around her grandmother's thin legs and lean down to speak in a quiet tone to the woman who displayed no recognition of her granddaughter or responded in any way. Since it was obvious that Meghan was unaware of his presence, he considered announcing that he was just a few feet from where they were as he heard her begin to speak again.

"I'm sorry I didn't get here last night as I'd planned, Grandma. I had to work late."

He watched Meghan's loose dark hair veil her face as she leaned to kiss her grandmother's cheek. "But I wouldn't miss your birthday. Isn't it a gorgeous day? Is the sun too bright for your eyes? Deanna gave me your hat in case you needed it."

Although Geoffrey felt like an intruder observing yet not revealing his presence, he was held spellbound as he watched the two Blake women together. One was a youthful, successful, energetic woman with a clear vision of her

future, and the other a weak, unresponsive individual without plans for the next minute. The contrast saddened him.
With quiet movements, he closed the glass door and stepped
back into the living room.

"I never count on you for anything anymore."

Meghan watched Sarah finger the pewter photograph
frame on the desk in the beach house den. As usual, they
were arguing again.

"Zach thought it was strange that you didn't even bother to
call last night but, overall, we managed just fine without you."

Sarah rounded the corner of the desk and, for a fleeting
moment, Meghan wondered if their relationship could have
been better if she had put more effort into getting to know
Sarah over the years and trying to understand her.

Sarah was so different from Meghan; she had little interest in Blake Industries, while Meghan's whole life revolved
around the business. Sarah had numerous friends and was
plagued every weekend with the decision of which party or
social gathering to attend. Meghan, on the other hand, had
few acquaintances who were not business associates and no
real friends, no one in whom she could confide. After so
many missed play opening nights, dance recitals and school
events, Sarah had stopped letting work be an excuse for
Meghan's lack of presence in her life.

Under the circumstances, Meghan could hardly blame her.

"I have to go and get ready. Zach and I have friends coming. A lot of them are staying until Monday because of the
long holiday weekend. Grandma's guests are coming around
seven for cocktails. You'll be here when she cuts her cake,
won't you?"

Meghan looked up from the computer screen on her desk.
"Yes, I plan to be here, Sarah."

"I'm sure you'll be pleased to know that Zach's uncle

agrees with you about our engagement. He's practically accused me of using my relationship with Zach to get information about some Wright family pharmaceutical company. Isn't that the most unbelievable thing you've ever heard?"

Sarah's comment caught Meghan's attention. "Did you know that Zach's uncle was Geoffrey Wright?" The tone of her question held more accusation than she had intended.

"Of course, I knew his name and who he was. Zach and I have no secrets from each other."

"Did you know that Blake Industries was interested in a particular Wright family firm?"

Sarah's green eyes widened. "Not you, too? You've got to be joking, Meghan. You certainly don't know me at all if you think that I would waste one second of my time on anything remotely connected with business."

Meghan rose from her chair. "I'm sorry, Sarah. I really had no idea that Geoffrey Wright was Zach's uncle." She reached out and squeezed her sister's hand. "He did seem to know that I was your sister."

Sarah grinned. "Everyone knows who you are, Meghan. It's hardly a secret that you're a very prominent member of the business community all over the country and even abroad. I'm sure he knows all about you."

Meghan shook her head. "I still can't believe it. I never made the connection."

"See, you work too hard. If you bothered to stop and listen to me once in a while, you might learn a few things." She gave Meghan a quick embrace. "Come on. We're all going out to the pool for a swim."

"You know I don't swim."

"Well, come out and sit in the sun. That pale skin of yours could use a little color. You're so white you look sick."

The telephone rang. For a moment, Meghan considered letting the answering machine take the call, but then she pulled her gaze away from Sarah's crestfallen face and reached for the receiver.

"Hi, Carly. I'm glad you called. I was just going to fax to the office my notes from the meeting with Sanford-Buckley."

"I'm really sorry to bother you today, Miss Blake; but something has come up of which I thought you should be informed of immediately. Arnold Bowman of Bowman Productions has arrived and is requesting an informal meeting this afternoon with several of the vice presidents. I have been able to reach Joseph Cohen and Robert Farley, but I haven't had any luck finding Jose Cortes or Diane Bennett. Didn't Jose go to Santa Domingo this weekend?'

"Yes, he is attending a family wedding. I have a few emergency numbers for Diane. I'll take care of calling her. What time does Mr. Bowman want to meet?"

"One o'clock at the Fair Oaks Country Club in Norfolk."

"Okay, Carly. I'll contact Diane. Can you make the meeting?"

"I'll try, but right now I'm stuck in Houston waiting to board my flight."

"Don't worry. Get there when you can. I'll drive up to Norfolk and help out with the meeting until everyone arrives." Meghan watched Sarah throw her another angry look and then stomp from the den. Meghan hung up the telephone.

A few minutes after five on Saturday afternoon, Meghan parked her car underneath her family's beach house and turned off the ignition. The meeting in Norfolk had been productive but draining, and the two-and-a-half hour drive to and from Hatteras Island twice in less than twenty-four hours had left her tired and restless.

Despite her exhaustion, she could not help wondering

what everyone at the beach had been doing while she was absent. The image of Geoffrey Wright emerging from the clear depths of the pool that morning was etched in her mind, and no matter how hard she tried, she could not dispel it. His wet hair, inquisitive gray eyes and serious mouth filled her thoughts. His smooth, tan skin glistening with water droplets in the early morning light and his low voice urging her to join him had shocked her so much that she was sure her heart had stopped beating.

What was it about Geoffrey Wright that wreaked havoc in her body? What had he done all afternoon? Where was he now? Did she want to see him?

"Meghan, you're back." Deanna Fuller, her grandmother's nurse, met her as Meghan stepped into the kitchen to get a glass of ice water. "I think Hilary has been wondering where you are. She's actually been calling out for you."

"She has? Is she in her room?"

The nurse nodded. "I think she'd like to go over to the beach. Sarah and Zach and their friends are all out there playing volleyball. Your grandmother would enjoy the action and noise."

"Isn't it too hot?"

"I don't think so, as long as she sits under an umbrella and doesn't stay out too long."

With Deanna's assistance, Meghan pushed Hilary along the boardwalk to the beach and set the elderly woman's wheelchair at an angle from which she could watch the volleyball game. She adjusted a large umbrella to shade her from the late afternoon sun. Unfolding a large towel, Meghan laid it next to her grandmother. Kicking off her sandals, she sank down onto it. She was so tired. She just wanted to sleep, but she forced a smile on her face and gave Hilary's hand a gentle squeeze.

"They're being awfully silly out there, aren't they, Grandma? I think they're breaking a few game rules."

There was no response in Hilary's eyes, and Meghan pulled her gaze back to her sister's friends, willing the burning tears in her own eyes to stop before they started falling down her cheeks and embarrassed her. When she saw Geoffrey approach them, she felt her heart quicken, and she inhaled a long deep breath of sea air.

"Good afternoon, ladies." He nodded to them as he squatted on the other side of her grandmother's wheelchair. "How was your drive to Norfolk? Sarah said you had a meeting."

"I'm sure she did not hide her indignation when she told you."

Geoffrey chuckled. "I suppose I should be grateful to you. Although I didn't think it possible, your sister has been more upset at you than at me today. You and I seem to have an uncanny knack for irritating the younger members of our families."

"It's a skill I've mastered through the years. Apparently, according to Sarah, I'm quite good at it."

His gray eyes smiled at her, and Meghan felt her heart skip a beat. With effort, she forced her gaze back to the volleyball game. They watched in silence as the ball was passed back and forth over the net by laughing, shouting college students. When the ball fell and rolled near the umbrella, Geoffrey reached for it.

A slight movement of Hilary Blake's right hand caused both Meghan and Geoffrey to look at the elderly woman. "What is it, Grandma? Do you want to go back to the house?"

Geoffrey caught her eye and winked. "Do you want the ball, Mrs. Blake?" He set the volleyball in her lap. "Is this what you want?"

Meghan gasped as Hilary clutched the ball with her right

hand. She met Geoffrey's gray eyes and could not help but smile. "Years ago, she used to love to play volleyball here on the beach. She and Grandpa and their friends would all get together in the summer and hold their own unofficial tournaments."

"Send it back over, will you, Geoff?" one of the players shouted from his position near the net.

"The kids need their ball back, Mrs. Blake. Let's give it a good toss, shall we? Here, let me help you."

Meghan watched in amazement as her grandmother nudged the ball toward Geoffrey's outstretched hands. The elderly woman made neither eye contact nor a single sound, but Meghan was sure Hilary had some sense of awareness of the game and her role as spectator.

"Oh, Grandma." Her words were a whisper as she rose to her knees to kiss her grandmother's thin, wrinkled cheek. Uninhibited by the sudden burst of joy, she allowed tears to flow with ease down her cheeks. "I'm so glad you're having a good time."

Squeezing her grandmother's hands before sitting back down on the towel, Meghan stole a quick glance at Geoffrey whose attention was already focused on the spirited game. She studied his profile, his strong determined jaw line and clean-shaven face, his straight narrow nose, his thick dark brown hair sprinkled with just a touch of silver at each temple. His relaxed and serene appearance, as he squatted there on the sand with his tanned hand resting on the arm of her grandmother's wheelchair, gave Meghan an odd sense of tranquility that she rarely experienced in her demanding life.

The feelings made her very uncomfortable, and she forced her eyes to focus on Sarah and Zach and their friends enjoying the hot summer day. Soon, the young people deserted the volleyball in favor of a game of tag at the edge of the water.

The splashing and squealing created a lively and noisy scene; but, Meghan noted, her grandmother displayed no reaction. She hoped Hilary was happy. It was just so hard to tell.

Meghan turned when she heard someone walking along the nearby boardwalk. Seeing her grandmother's nurse, she rose to her feet.

"Well, it looks like you folks are having a good time out here." Deanna Fuller moved to stand in front of the wheel-chair. "Are you enjoying this wonderful day, Hilary? Meghan and Mr. Wright are keeping you company, I see."

The nurse turned to Meghan. "It's time for her medicine, and she's probably had enough sun for the day. She should have a little rest before her party later. I'll take you back to the house, Hilary, so Meghan can stay here at the beach."

Meghan shook her head. "No, thanks, Deanna. I'd like to walk back with Grandma. We'll meet you back there in a few minutes." The hot moist breeze caressed her skin as she stepped from beneath the shade of the umbrella. Yawning, she stretched her exhausted arms toward the bright blue sky.

"You look tired, Meghan."

Geoffrey's low voice startled her. "I am," she said without thinking. Irritated with herself for allowing him to unnerve her as he did, she tossed him a smile and tucked her towel into a pouch in the back of her grandmother's wheelchair. "Ready to go, Grandma?"

Her heart quickened as he touched her arm. "Let me help."

She stepped aside as he guided Hilary's chair onto the ramp to the boardwalk. As she watched his muscles contract and relax below the short sleeves of his T-shirt and strands of his dark hair flutter in the sea breeze, a sense of warmth flooded over her. Geoffrey's kindness toward her grand-mother impressed her more than any business skills he may have demonstrated. Every man she had dated since her grandmother had been diagnosed with Alzheimer's disease had avoided any contact with, or discussion of, Hilary or her condition.

As she reached for the handles of the wheelchair, her fingers brushed against his. She could not deny the momentary tremor jolting through her hand and up her arm as she came into physical contact with his warm skin. She swallowed the lump forming in her throat. "Thank you."

He smiled down at her. "Are you sure you don't want help? I don't mind walking back with you."

She shook her head. "I'll be fine." Her hands trembled as he continued to look at her. "What?"

Reaching out, he tucked a strand of hair behind her ear. "Don't work too hard, Meghan. You need a little fun in your life."

She sighed as she tried to ignore the sudden increase in her heart beat. "That's what Sarah says."

Two hours later, Meghan stood next to her grandmother, who was seated at a table piled high with gifts and a sheet cake decorated with fresh summer flowers. On her other side stood Sarah, arm in arm with Zach. As she completed a second verse of "Happy Birthday" with the guests, Meghan noted that Sarah and Zach appeared to enjoy each other's company; but, she thought, there was more to life than fun. Sarah could not imagine the potential hardships of life after college, or the demands and challenges of making a living when someone else was depending on her. No, her naive younger sister had little knowledge of what lay ahead of her, especially if she decided to go through with her plans to marry Zach.

As Deanna accompanied Hilary to a nearby table to help the elderly woman eat a piece of birthday cake, Meghan's eyes scanned the various guests mingling in small groups around the room. Friends of the Blake family, and business associates who had known her father and grandfather, talked in muted voices among themselves or stopped to say a few congratulatory words to her grandmother.

For a moment, Meghan's eyes rested on the back of a man in navy blue pants and a light sports jacket. She could not see his face, but his dark thick hair sprinkled with silver, and the relaxed, yet confident, stance of his muscular body caused her to recognize him in an instant. Despite her resolve to ignore him, she could not deny that he was an attractive man. Before she could pull away her gaze, his gray eyes locked with hers from across the room. Forcing a casual smile on her lips, she strode toward him and the man with whom he was talking.

"Meghan, there you are." The large burly man in a wrinkled linen suit smiled at her. "Marvelous party, just marvelous. As your invitation suggested, I've made a donation in your grandmother's name to the Blake Family Foundation of Hampton Roads in lieu of a gift. I'll be there for the spring Walk for a Cure next June, and you can count on me and my company to make a significant contribution. Anything for John Blake's mother."

Meghan nodded. "Thank you, Mr. Gates. That's very generous of you."

"I'm afraid I have to leave, my dear. I have a dinner engagement in Portsmouth this evening, but I'll say goodbye to Hilary before I leave. It was nice to see you again, Meghan."

As the older man walked away from them, she felt suddenly tongue tied. Why did being with Geoffrey Wright create such havoc with her emotions? Swallowing, she experienced the vague awareness of a sore throat developing as she realized she could not ignore the question on Geoffrey's face. To avoid those perceptive gray eyes, she turned to look at her grandmother. "I set up the Foundation when Grandma was first diagnosed. I felt, well, powerless. I had to do something." With a racing heart, she watched guests surrounding her grandmother and taking turns wishing her well. She wondered how much of the whole event the older woman understood.

"Blake Industries sponsors the spring Walk for a Cure every year?"

The sound of his quiet voice calmed her unsteady nerves. With a nod, she turned to look at him and was surprised by the compassion she saw in the depths of his gray eyes. Was it possible that he cared for her grandmother? They had been strangers until yesterday. Was Geoffrey's heart so full that he could feel empathy toward people he did not even know—individuals like Hilary, whose severe medical condition often disgusted or frightened others? Meghan often encountered scared and uncaring people, but she rarely met any with unconditional kindness to give.

Unable to explain why she did it, she reached out and squeezed his hand. Electricity surged through her and took away her breath. He responded to her spontaneous act by lacing his fingers with hers as he turned to gaze across the room at Hilary.

She inhaled a deep breath. What was she doing? She could not be drawn to Geoffrey's charm and thoughtfulness. She had no time for friendship, and even less time for romantic ideas of love.

"Your grandmother certainly seems to be enjoying herself."

Smiling, Meghan pulled her hand from his grasp. "If you'll excuse me, I think I'll go check on her. She's probably getting tired from all of this attention."

Meghan did not see Geoffrey again until she entered the dining room later that evening. The late informal supper to celebrate Sarah and Zach's engagement had already begun when she finished her call from her executive assistant and finally joined the younger couple's guests. They had made their selections from the generous dishes of seafood, fresh fruit and vegetables on the buffet, and were now seated together at the table laughing, joking, eating and enjoying each other's company.

Stepping through the arched doorway, Meghan attempted to enter the room without announcement; but Geoffrey, seated across from Sarah and Zach near the end of the table, beckoned to her with his hand and indicated an empty seat next to him. The sight of him smiling at her, in his dark pleated pants and white oxford shirt unbuttoned at the neck, caused her heart to race.

Stop acting like a high school student drooling over the varsity football captain, she told herself. Swallowing the lump in her throat, she directed her unsteady legs toward the table. *Remember, he's a business rival. Stop thinking about how attractive he is.*

"So you finally decided to show up." Sarah's whispered, yet cutting, words jabbed at the guilt already stabbing her stomach.

"Don't, Sarah." She saw Zach squeeze her sister's hand. "She's here now."

"Come, join us, Meghan." Geoffrey rose to pull a chair out for her. "I was just preparing to make a toast."

A toast? She definitely did not want to drink anything with alcohol. Her throat hurt too much. She swallowed a wave of nausea. Was she sick?

She tried to make sense of what was happening. The room felt warm, and she had the sensation that the walls were closing in on her where she sat. She heard several soft rings as guests tapped their glasses with silverware. The room fell silent, and Meghan was aware of Geoffrey standing up next to her as his voice requested everyone's attention. She closed her eyes to the dull ache at her temples. With only vague concentration, she tried to listen to Geoffrey's words. What was he saying? Why did she find it so difficult to focus on a simple toast?

"I'm sure that everyone here enjoying the hospitality of the Blake family tonight knows why we are celebrating. Sarah Blake has kindly accepted the proposal of marriage made by my nephew, Zachary. They have decided to have a fall wedding, at a time and place yet to be determined. I would like to take this opportunity to congratulate Sarah and Zach, and to give our best wishes and lend our support as they begin their future as husband and wife."

Chapter Five

As Meghan struggled to focus on his words, he turned to look down at her. "Would you like to add anything, Meghan?"

She knew she needed to concentrate. She did not want to hurt Sarah or to embarrass herself in front of all of the strangers sitting around the table waiting for her to speak. *The engagement*! Geoffrey had asked her to say something about Sarah and Zach's engagement.

She rose from her seat. Her head throbbed as she glanced around the table at the eyes of every guest resting on her. When she cleared her throat, she was astonished by the irritation the action caused all the way down the length of it.

"I would like to join Geoffrey in offering my best wishes to Sarah and Zach on the announcement of their engagement."

Clapping and words of congratulations filled her ears as she slumped back into her chair. Sights and sounds whirled around her head in confusion. She could concentrate on nothing but the spinning room and her throbbing head. Clutching the lace edge of the table cloth, she inhaled short quick breaths of air. Nausea tumbled in her stomach, and her throat burned. As she attempted to sort out what was happening to her, she felt a warm hand touch her arm. When she turned her head and forced her eyes on his face, she was comforted by the expression of concern in Geoffrey Wright's eyes.

"What's wrong, Meghan? Are you all right?" His voice was almost a whisper and close to her ear, as though he realized how important it was to her not to arouse the attention of the other guests. She wished *he* had not noticed, but it was too late for that.

He folded his hand around hers. "Your fingers are like ice."

"It's the food and the smells and the noise." She barely recognized her own voice. "I think I should leave." She slid her chair back from the table and rose to her feet.

As she began to stumble toward the doorway, Geoffrey hurried to her side. With swift, fluid movements, he slipped his arm around her waist and guided her out of the room. The din of the occupants talking in the dining room began to subside, and Meghan inhaled a deep, steady breath.

"I'm okay. Thank you." She tried to ignore her pounding temples and irritated throat. She focused her eyes on the spinning living room.

"Come, sit down." Despite her distress, she liked his quiet voice as he grasped her elbow with a gentle, supportive hold. Leading her to a nearby chair, he eased her down onto its soft cushion. He seemed to know she needed uninterrupted silence, because he sat on the edge of the sofa and waited without a word while she willed the room to stop spinning and her head to stop pounding.

After several moments, she nodded and gave him a weak smile. "I don't quite know what's wrong. I guess I'm feeling a little light headed."

"Have you eaten?"

The intense gaze of his piercing eyes bore into her soul,

and she looked away to stare at the expanse of moonlit beach through the sliding glass doors. "I've been so busy all day."

"I'll get you something." He rose to his feet.

"No, no. I'm better now." His eyes appeared able to see through her most convincing words. "Really, Geoffrey."

The telephone in her skirt pocket rang. Pulling it out, she raised it to her ear. "It's my executive assistant. Please excuse me, but I have to take this call."

When he hesitated, standing just inches from her with his muscular chest that had glistened with water earlier that day, her heart skipped a beat. She inhaled a steady breath of air that included the spicy scent of his cologne and said, "Go back to the party."

"Not until you promise me you'll have something to eat as soon as you finish your phone call."

Why did it matter to him? She was so unaccustomed to anyone being concerned about her personal needs that the realization that Geoffrey Wright cared made her uncomfortable. Aware that he waited while her call did, too, she nodded. "I promise. Now, go."

Hours later, Meghan rubbed the back of her neck and yawned. The figures on the spreadsheet on the computer monitor in front of her blurred before her eyes. Glancing at the small clock near her desk blotter, she was surprised that it was nearly 2:00 in the morning. She took a sip of warm water, then turned her attention back to her work. Despite her intention to complete the report on which she was working, she knew she needed sleep; but she also realized that if she did go to bed, she would not rest. Her mind was too full of worries about Sarah, about her sore throat and throbbing head, and about the unnerving presence of Geoffrey Wright.

As if on cue, she heard his quiet voice. Was she hallucinating now?

"Do you ever sleep?"

Holding her breath, she pulled her eyes away from the computer and looked toward the open door. Outlined by the pale birch frame stood Geoffrey's tall figure. His plaid pajama bottoms fell to his ankles and exposed long tanned feet while his matching robe, tied at the waist, revealed a triangular spot of tanned skin and dark chest hair at his neck line.

He stuffed his hands into his robe pockets and leaned against the open doorway. "You're not feeling well, Meghan. Why aren't you resting?"

"You're not resting either." She raised her eyebrows. "Couldn't you sleep?"

He shrugged his broad shoulders. "I guess I've been thinking about Zach and Sarah. I can't help worrying about this big step they're taking."

Pain throbbed at her temples. "Was your toast not as sincere as it sounded?"

He shook his head. "No, of course not. I meant every word. Although I have my doubts, I'm convinced that they are in love and serious about getting married."

She reached for her glass of water. "And if they *are* making a big mistake?"

He walked across the tiled floor and sat down in one of the easy chairs near her desk. "Their love will make their marriage successful."

She traced the intricate etching on the crystal glass with the tip of her finger. "How can you be so sure love exists?"

"Because my nephew and your sister say it does. My mother says we have to trust them."

She met his intense gray eyes. "Trusting others is not one of my stronger assets."

"It isn't one of mine either, I'm afraid." His smile helped to ease some of Meghan's worried thoughts. She watched him as he continued. "I believe true love can exist if a deep enduring emotional bond develops between two people who care selflessly for one another."

"And you think that Sarah and Zach possess the capacity for that kind of selflessness?"

He nodded. "They need our support now, not our unsubstantiated suspicions and personal doubts based on past experiences of our own."

She pulled her gaze from him as she considered his words. He was so casual and direct with her. It was refreshing and unnerving all at the same time.

"How is your throat feeling?"

The tone of his voice was soft and soothing. She had mentioned her sore throat to no one. How could he have been aware of it?

"My throat?"

"I noticed earlier that you seemed to be having trouble swallowing. Is it still bothering you?"

"No, of course not. I'm fine." She avoided the question as she turned back to the spreadsheet on her computer. She was not sure she liked the way he looked at her, the way his intense gray eyes studied her or the way he seemed to read her mind. She watched him reach for a picture framed in antique pewter on the corner of her desk.

"I'm guessing that this photograph is one of you as a child. About ten years old?"

It was one of very few photos she had of her father and the only one she had of her older brother. She swallowed the lump in her throat. "Eleven."

"Is this your father?"

"The one holding the sea bass."

"And the young boy?"

Hot tears stung her eyes. Geoffrey Wright asked too many questions. "My brother." She brushed her face with her hands before glancing at him around the edge of her computer monitor.

He looked surprised. "I didn't know you had other siblings."

"I don't. He was my older brother, John Jr. We called him Jay."

"John Blake had a son?"

"He died a few weeks after that picture was taken."

She watched his eyes lift from the photograph to meet her gaze. What did she see there? Sadness? Kindness? Empathy? Her heart skipped a few beats in spite of her resolve to ignore his intense presence.

"Oh, I had no idea. I'm sorry."

"It was a long time ago."

She turned back to the computer screen as tears spilled from her eyes. She heard him replace the photograph on her desk. As the usual distress and grief of the memory of Jay's death enveloped her, she experienced an odd sense of tranquility in the silence that hung between them in the den. What kind of power did Geoffrey Wright have over her that created such comfort as she relived her sorrow?

"Well, I should go and let you finish your work." He rose to his feet. "Good night, Meghan. I hope your throat feels better."

"I don't mind, Meghan. I'll just take this afternoon off and go to Ocracoke to visit my family then."

"No, Deanna." Meghan's head was still throbbing the following morning as she gave it a firm shake. "You need to take some time off. You deserve the whole day. Maybe Sarah will be willing to drive the van."

"Good morning, ladies." Geoffrey Wright smiled as he entered the dining room, where Meghan and Deanna had just joined a few of the weekend guests at the breakfast table. His gray eyes glistened with cheerful geniality on his handsome, tanned face as he nodded to them.

"You look bright and rested this morning, Mr. Wright. It's too bad it's such a dreary day outside."

He accepted a steaming cup of coffee from the maid and took a seat next to Deanna and across from Meghan, who pulled her gaze away from his inquisitive eyes. His dark hair, still damp from a shower, shone in the soft light from the pair of powder coated wrought iron chandeliers above their heads. She wondered if he had already gone swimming. Without much effort, she could imagine his bronze, athletic body skimming along the surface of the water.

"Ah, but it's not raining."

"Not yet, anyway." Deanna turned back to Meghan. "I don't like the idea of you going alone with Hilary down to Buxton. I'll take you."

Meghan handed her grandmother's nurse a plate of toast. "I've made up my mind. Today is your day off, and it's Independence Day. Go have fun with your family."

Geoffrey cleared his throat and Meghan turned to look at him. "Excuse me for listening, but I'd like to offer you my help. I would be more than happy to accompany you and your grandmother, if you need assistance."

"Yes, she does." Deanna appeared to ignore Meghan's warning glare. "Thank you, Mr. Wright. Meghan is determined to take her grandmother down to Buxton while still insisting that I not change my plans to spend the day with my family in Ocracoke. It would be a big relief to me if you could drive the van for her and help Hilary in and out of it."

Geoffrey smiled, flashing perfect, white teeth. "That's no problem at all. Just let me finish my coffee, and I'll be ready. What time did you want to go?"

Meghan opened her mouth to protest, but the pain in her swollen throat and pounding head stopped her. Maybe having him along would not be so bad. She really did not trust herself to drive with her temples throbbing as they were, and her grandmother seemed to like the man who would very soon be Sarah's uncle by marriage.

With no energy to argue, she nodded. "I'll go help Grandma finish getting ready. We'll probably be leaving the house in about thirty minutes."

Meghan was grateful that Geoffrey did not try to talk with her on the drive of less than twenty miles down the island of Hatteras to the village of Buxton. At frequent intervals, she checked to see if her grandmother was comfortable, and to point out to the elderly woman something of interest along the ocean or sound side of the road.

A few times, she felt Geoffrey's eyes on her. When she turned to look at him, she was always surprised by the warmth of his smile.

"This island has such natural beauty and tranquility." His words were quiet and seemed sincere. "I could easily forget all of life's concerns just staying here."

To forget all of life's concerns. What an incredible idea!

She watched as he reduced his speed upon entering the village limits, then turned around to Hilary. "We're going to the Hatteras lighthouse, Grandma, just like you and I used to do every time we stayed on the Outer Banks. We're nearly there."

"Now, turn right?" Geoffrey made his way with care, at a slow speed along the paved road lined with trees and bushes.

"No, left."

"The sign indicates that the lighthouse is to the right."

She leaned toward him and lowered her voice. "But Grandma likes to go left."

He gave her a puzzled look. "Left it is. Here we are, Mrs. Blake." Geoffrey pulled the van into an empty parking area and turned off the ignition. "We're lucky the rain is holding off for us."

Meghan watched Geoffrey gaze out at the thick dark layer of clouds hanging over the ocean, beyond the sand dunes and waving sea oats. "That sky looks spooky."

He turned to her. "A storm is coming?"

She opened the side door of the van and activated a handicap accessible ramp. "I heard on the news this morning that a tropical storm is hitting some islands in the Caribbean. We'll probably have to deal with wind and rain from that storm system here on the North Carolina coast." She pushed her grandmother onto the platform and secured the wheelchair with metal clamps before pushing a button to lower the ramp to the ground.

Geoffrey had already rounded the front of the van and was standing near the ramp as it stopped, level with the pavement. He unclasped the wheelchair and pushed her grandmother a safe distance away from the vehicle while Meghan raised the platform and closed the handicap door before stepping out of the van herself with her briefcase in her hand.

"You're fairly adept with the equipment."

His eyes leveled on hers. "Running a company that designs and distributes adapted medical equipment and assistive technology has its advantages. I'm afraid I'd rather be testing and demonstrating products than sitting all day in conferences and meetings."

With a smile, he bent his head to whisper in her ear. "I don't see the lighthouse."

She breathed in his fresh, clean, masculine scent and wished her heart would stop its erratic beat. "It's over beyond those trees." She pointed to the right of the parking area.

"Didn't you tell your grandmother we were going to the lighthouse?"

"This is the spot where it used to be, where we used to come together. A few years ago, the Cape Hatteras lighthouse had to be moved because its stability was being threatened by erosion of the land on which it was set." She indicated an area of grass and sand a hundred feet beyond the parking area, and Geoffrey began pushing Hilary's wheelchair toward it. "Grandma always loved this spot. When I was a little girl, she often brought me down here. Sometimes, we'd climb the steps to the top of the lighthouse or walk over to the beach or just sit and talk here in the shadow of the great beacon, that for many years has been warning ships of the danger of nearby shoals and coastline."

He stopped and turned her grandmother's chair toward the dunes. "So, you and she continue the tradition?"

Meghan lifted her face to allow the breeze to blow through her loose hair and play with the full skirt of her sleeveless cotton dress. "Before she became ill, she painted. She would set up her easel and her watercolors and create the most beautiful seascapes."

"Did you paint, too?"

Meghan laughed. "Me? No, I'm afraid Sarah received all of the creative genes in our family. While Grandma painted, I used to read or talk with her or pick up shells on the beach."

"So, what do you plan to do this morning?"

She sat down on the grass a few feet from her grandmother. "I was going to proofread some reports, but I think I'll just sit and take a few notes for upcoming meetings."

She wished the throbbing at her temples would stop. Reading was almost impossible when she could barely focus her eyes. She held her breath as Geoffrey eased down next to her on the grass. She watched the muscles of his chest and arms contract and expand under the knitted fabric of the blue polo shirt that topped his navy pants. *With all of the grass available, could he not have chosen another spot on which to sit?*

After giving her grandmother's hand a light squeeze; she unzipped her briefcase and pulled out a pen and small yellow legal pad. As she began to write, she was acutely aware of the dark, quiet man next to her.

"Do you think your grandmother is aware of her surroundings?" His voice was soft and barely audible above the rustle of leaves and the surf.

Meghan stopped writing and gazed out at the ocean waves beating against the beach. "I don't know. I hope she is, sometimes, anyway. She seemed to be quite aware of the volleyball game yesterday, but she has made no sign of recognizing Sarah or me in almost two months."

"It must be heartbreaking for you."

She turned to look at him. Why must he be so kind and perceptive? How could she be expected to hold her feelings in check against his constant onslaught of compassion? Tears spilled from her eyes and slipped down her cheeks before she could stop them. "I'm sorry." Her words were a whisper. "I'm not usually so emotional."

He draped a strong muscular arm around her shoulders, and warmth and comfort covered her like a blanket. "Don't apologize for your feelings, Meghan. Just accept them. You have every right to cry."

"Crying isn't very becoming." She sniffled, and he handed her a clean white handkerchief that smelled of his musky masculinity.

"It's part of life, a part of you." He gave her shoulders a gentle squeeze. "Putting up a pretense is certainly not necessary when you're with me. We're practically related."

Related? Yes, she supposed they were, almost, but was it not even more necessary to mask her feelings from family members? Her father had always discouraged her from the time she was a little girl from displaying such emotional outbursts.

For a moment, she allowed herself to enjoy the security and solace of his embrace before wiping her eyes and pulling away from him. She could not permit herself to grow accustomed to the comfort he offered. In silence, she turned her attention to her notes again. Although he did not speak, she was well aware of Geoffrey's nearness.

Almost an hour later, she glanced at her wrist watch. "We probably should be getting back. I don't want you to tire out too much, Grandma."

"You look quite tired yourself, Meghan." He grasped her elbow to steady her as she rose to her feet beside him.

"Just a little, I suppose." She wished he was not so observant or so solicitous or so tall. She inhaled a deep breath of sea air. "What are your plans for the remainder of the day?"

He maneuvered the wheelchair around on the grass and headed back toward the van as she fell in step beside him. "Sarah and Zach invited me to go wind-surfing with them and their friends in Pamlico Sound." Although his pace was a leisurely one, Geoffrey's legs were so long that Meghan had a difficult time keeping up with him. "Would you like to join us?"

"Oh, no, thank you. Since Deanna has the day off, Grandma and I are going to keep each other company."

The rest of the day was very quiet. With Sarah and her guests gone for the afternoon, Meghan took Hilary to the den while she worked. They had a simple lunch together on the screen porch adjacent to the living room; and while her grandmother napped in her bedroom, Meghan sat next to her bed and looked over reports.

When Deanna returned to the beach house at 5:00 and relieved her, Meghan drove to her office in Newport News to take care of some details for a regional meeting of her vice presidents scheduled for later that week in Richmond. Although her throat still hurt, the aspirin she took helped ease the pain in her head enough to make driving and reading bearable. She hoped that the sickness she had would run its course without too much interruption in her routine. It was so hard to concentrate with a nagging headache and swollen throat.

When she finally drove back to her family's vacation home on Hatteras Island, the night was dark, and the wind was strong and fierce. The house itself was quiet, except for the frequent gusts outside, whipping and howling around the unprotected island.

She had missed dinner; the kitchen was clean and empty. Knowing Sarah would be upset that she had missed yet another meal that weekend, and dreading the inevitable argument that would follow, she headed straight for the den—she hoped to avoid her sister, at least for a little while. She had just settled down behind the desk when she heard approaching footsteps.

Geoffrey Wright. She smiled in spite of her exhaustion, persistent physical ailments and worries about disappointing Sarah. Removing the sweater she had worn over her casual sun dress, she opened her briefcase and looked up at the tall figure in the doorway of the den. "How was the wind-surfing?"

"Breathtaking, exhilarating, an unforgettable experience—you should have joined us." He returned her smile, and her heart skipped a beat.

Meghan laughed, and she was astonished by the sound. How long had it been since she had laughed aloud? "I'm glad to hear that you had such a good time. And Zach and Sarah? Did they have fun, too?"

In lightweight pants, a worn oxford shirt and leather loafers, he strode across the oriental carpet and took a seat in an easy chair in front of her desk. "Yes, they appeared to enjoy the afternoon immensely. I'm convinced that they would relish collecting week old garbage as long as they could do it together."

She grinned at the thought of her neat, groomed sister tossing trash bags into the back of a foul smelling truck. "So, that's what love is?"

Chuckling, he shrugged his broad shoulders. "It's undeniable that they have discovered some kind of magic."

She studied him as he relaxed in the chair with his long right leg crossed over his left knee. She wondered if it were possible that his bronze skin had become even more tanned on such a cloudy day.

"We all wished you had come with us. Sarah kept commenting on your wind-surfing expertise as a youth."

"I was reckless and immature."

"Your sister thinks you were daring and fearless. She admires you, Meghan."

She met his eyes. "You must be mistaken. Sarah has little respect for anything I do."

His eyes held hers, even though she wanted to pull her gaze away from their intensity. "On the contrary, I think you underestimate the depth of your sister's affection." He leaned forward in his chair and rested his elbows on her desk. "Perhaps you worry too much about the way you think family members should interact. You and Sarah can share a close and satisfying relationship without always agreeing on everything."

"You and Zach seem to agree on most issues."

"Not on everything. You and I have had similar experiences, I suppose, because we have been thrown into the dif-

ficult position, without benefit of age or experience, of raising young individuals into adulthood. It is an important yet,
at times, demanding and stressful obligation. Fortunately,
I've had my mother, to whom I could always turn for advice
and guidance. You have had no one since your grandmother
became ill." He smiled at her. "Maybe you should try not to
be so critical of Sarah and the decisions she makes. My
mother has reminded me that everyone needs to make his
own mistakes in life."

Meghan sighed as she considered his words. "I'm afraid I
haven't been a very good sister or parent to Sarah. I guess
she was destined to lose out in life."

He shook his head. "Don't be so hard on yourself, my
dear. You were given an awesome responsibility when your
father died. Not only did you have to head his company, but
you had to raise his adolescent daughter, who, more than
likely, has tried to sway your better judgment on more than
one occasion to get what she wanted, because that's what
kids do."

His quiet voice encouraged her in a way she had not known
she needed. His words seemed to lighten the heaviness she
had been hiding in her heart. Who was this man who gave her
everything she required even before she realized she lacked it?

"I don't know what to do. I know Sarah's upset with me
right now because I missed another family meal."

He chuckled. " 'Upset' might be a slight understatement
right now."

"I guess I owe her an apology."

Gray eyes full of kindness and understanding leveled on
hers. "An apology is certainly a start."

"I'm not sure I can change."

"You're reasonable and determined, and you care about
your sister. You can change if you try." He smiled. "Spend

more time with Sarah. Don't be afraid to show her you love her. That's all it takes."

"That's all? What you're suggesting seems monumental."

"I have no doubt in my mind that you'll succeed, Meghan."

Why did she value this man's declaration of confidence? She sighed. "Where are Sarah and Zach now?"

"Downstairs, playing pool."

"Sarah loves to play. You didn't want to join them?"

He grinned at her from across the large desk top. "Actually, your sister asked me to try to persuade you to come down."

"I'm too old for games."

"Age has nothing to do with one's ability to have fun or, for that matter, one's need to relax, on occasion." He pointed to the picture on her desk. "I see by this photo that there was a time when you had fun."

She stared at it for several silent moments. Without thinking, she pressed her fingers to her temples as another pulse of pain pounded against her brain.

"Is your head hurting too?"

With quick movements she pulled her hands down into her lap and squeezed them together. "I'm just a little tired."

"You really need to learn to relax." He rose from his chair and rounded the desk toward her.

What was he doing? She held her breath as she felt his hands curve around the thin cotton fabric covering her shoulders.

"I'm trying to massage the tension out of your neck. You're a bundle of nerves, Meghan."

Her heart raced as the movement of his hands sent warmth flooding down her arms. His touch was tender, and offered a release of tension she had not imagined possible. "Don't." Her voice whispered the ineffective plea.

"Why not?" His thumbs caressed the base of her neck with gentle, circular motions.

"Because I'll get too comfortable."

"What's wrong with comfortable?"

"It feels too good. It distracts me from my work."

"That's the basic idea of relaxing."

"I'm serious, Geoffrey. I have hours of work to do this evening."

"I'm serious too. In my guarded opinion, you spend entirely too much time working, and not nearly enough time taking care of yourself." He surprised her by swinging her chair around until his gray eyes locked with hers. For a moment he held her gaze before taking her hands and urging her to her feet.

She felt heat flow from his touch. She wanted to pull away from him and feel his arms around her, all at the same time. Swallowing, she winced from the rawness in her throat. "What are you doing?"

"Seeing to it that you take a break." When she began to protest, he put a finger to her lips. "You need a break. You've either worked on reports, talked on the phone, or had meetings all weekend. It's a national holiday. Independence Day is a time to celebrate and to have fun with family and friends." He draped her sweater over her shoulders and then slipped his arm around her waist. Guiding her around the corner of her desk, he led her to the door.

"Where are we going?"

"I'm taking you away from all of this, my dear." He swept the air with his free arm. "Away from computers, telephones, calendars and agendas. I plan to treat you to the fun, relaxing and entertaining evening that you deserve."

"I can't."

"Why not?" He led her down to the parking area beneath the house. "Give me one convincing reason."

She tried to ignore the throbbing of her temples and the

pain along the length of her throat. "I don't have to give you a reason."

He stopped and gazed down at her as his arm around her waist continued to create intense warmth that circulated throughout her body. "You have a point, I suppose. You're under no obligation to accompany me."

She watched a smile tug at the edges of his mouth. His teasing eyes sent little flutters tumbling against the inside of her stomach. She wished her head would stop pounding for a few seconds until she regained her common sense.

"Meghan, please accept my invitation to dinner?"

"It's after ten."

"And you haven't eaten a decent meal all weekend." He opened the front door of his small rental car and waited for her to slide into the vehicle. "Come have something with me now."

Eating was the farthest thing from her mind, and she was about to protest when the parking area began to dip and spin before her eyes. She had no choice but to sink into the soft leather seat.

"I don't have my purse." She closed her eyes to the incessant drum beat in her head.

"You won't need it. Tonight is my treat."

He started the engine and waited while she fastened her seat belt before backing out into the quiet cul-de-sac. In minutes they were speeding along the dark, empty highway that ran the length of Hatteras Island.

"Sarah and Zach have mentioned some places that serve light meals anytime. Do you have a preference?"

"No." She shook her head and then pressed her temples with her fingertips. She hoped he did not expect her to engage in conversation all the way to Avon. Short responses to simple questions were about all she could manage at the moment.

To her relief, Geoffrey made a few comments about the island and the wide uninhabited stretch of land between villages, but did not insist on verbal responses from her. When the night lights of the approaching town came into view, Meghan leaned against the headrest of her seat and closed her eyes again. Why did she feel so sick? What was happening to her typical, well-planned life?

Chapter Six

Geoffrey pulled his car into the parking area of a popular Outer Banks restaurant and held the door for Meghan as she stepped out onto the gravel lot. A whirling high-pitched whistle pierced the air.

"Fireworks?"

Meghan nodded. "People set them off on the beaches all through the hot weather months."

Lively music and the sound of patrons celebrating at the bar and in the dance area drifted through the lobby as they entered, but Geoffrey requested a table in a small dining room toward the back of the building that offered both privacy and a quiet atmosphere. Despite the fact that most of the tables arranged around the dance floor were occupied, voices were hushed, and the music was low.

Meghan glanced around at the marine decor—fishing nets, crab and lobster traps, buoys, and a collection of fishing poles and reels. She still had not opened her menu when their server arrived to take their order. Noticing Geoffrey's patient waiting, she turned her attention to the heavy parchment; but the green print swam before her eyes.

As though he sensed her difficulty, he reached for her menu and turned to the server. "I think we'll have two turkey and Swiss cheese sandwiches with house salads. Is white bread okay, Meghan?"

When she nodded, he added, "And two tall glasses of orange juice, if you have it."

Although her sore throat felt swollen shut, the ice cold juice was less irritating than she expected, and she took small slow sips as Geoffrey's gray eyes studied her.

"It tastes good." She barely recognized her own voice when she spoke. It had become hoarse and raspy in just a few hours.

He took a drink from his own glass. "This place reminds me of a little bar and grill in Yarmouth, near my family's summer home."

"Sarah tells me you have a beach house on Cape Cod. When I was in college, I remember students driving out to Hyannis and Provincetown on the weekends. My roommate's family had a vacation home on Martha's Vineyard."

"A beautiful spot. Did you like it?"

"Yes, but I still prefer the beaches here." She shrugged her shoulders. "I guess I'll always be a southern girl at heart."

He smiled and reached across the table to hold her hand. "The proverbial southern belle, huh? A distinguished young business woman who also possesses the charm and beauty and social grace that accompany such a position in southern society."

Laughing, she shook her head. "Well, hardly all of that, but I do like to listen to the surf here, and enjoy escaping to Hatteras when I have the opportunity."

He rubbed her knuckles with the pad of his thumb. "It doesn't seem as though you've spent enough time here this weekend to accomplish that."

The tingling sensation created by his touch caused her

breath to quicken, and she slid her hand from his grasp. "I'm glad that you and Zach have had a chance to enjoy the island."

When the server arrived with their meals, she realized that she was hungry even though her throat was still sore and her head pounded in pain. She lifted her fork and speared a piece of lettuce and cucumber. With difficult and labored swallows, she managed to eat both her salad and then half of her sandwich. Having eaten all she could, she folded her napkin next to her plate as the server returned.

"May I offer you dessert or drink?"

Geoffrey turned to Meghan and waited for her response. When she shook her head, he said to the restaurant employee, "Just some decaffeinated coffee, please."

"What possible benefit does decaffeinated coffee provide?" She watched him pour a packet of sugar into the brewed liquid when it arrived.

He looked up at her as he stirred it. "I like the taste, but I don't like the way regular coffee ruins a good night of rest."

"I never drink decaf."

Leaning back in his chair, he nodded at her. "That's very likely the reason that you never sleep." His gaze was intense as he looked at her over the rim of his cup. Feeling uneasy about his silent attention, she pulled her eyes away to the small dance floor, where a couple swayed to a slow country melody flowing from the speakers of the jukebox near the door. "Would you like to dance?"

His question caused her breath to catch in her throat. With difficulty, she swallowed. "I don't dance. Sarah's the one with all of the grace and talent—and height."

"You don't have to be tall to enjoy dancing." Rising from his seat, he reached for her hand. "Come. Dance with me."

She tried to ignore the heat from his hand as it covered hers. Did she imagine a shock racing up her arm? Confused and unnerved, she rose and allowed him to guide her down the single step onto the dance floor, while being acutely aware of the gentle pressure of his hand against her lower back and the nearness of him.

She was surprised by the ease with which she fell into step with him as he led her around the floor with slow, flowing movements. Wishing her head did not hurt so much, she tried to concentrate on the rhythm of the beat—and avoiding his feet.

"So, tell me how you do it." His voice was so soft and mesmerizing. "What's your secret?'

She looked up into his searching gray eyes. "Secret to what?"

"You don't eat. You don't sleep. You don't allow yourself the typical distractions that others use to help themselves relax and unwind. How do you relieve the incredible tension that is an integral part of your career?"

She forced a smile. "I enjoy my work."

"Being the president of Blake Industries must place a tremendous burden on your personal life."

She stared at a point just above his broad shoulder and avoided his scrutinizing eyes. "I'm usually too busy to even miss a personal life."

"Do you ever wish you could be someone other than the head of a major multi-million dollar company?"

She smiled. "I don't think I could be anyone else. I wouldn't know how."

"Do you ever drop your protective shield of control and propriety and be just Meghan Blake, a young, attractive, intelligent woman?"

He smiled down at her. "Just be yourself. Be Meghan." He rubbed his hand up and down her back. "Relax. You're so stiff and tense." He lowered his head until it was close to her ear. "You may come closer, you know. I promise to be a perfect gentleman."

Her back tingled from his gentle rubbing, and she continued to feel the warmth of his breath on her ear long after he had raised his head. "I think I've had enough dancing." She stepped away from him.

"Are you feeling all right?"

She nodded. "I'm fine, but I'd just like to go home now."

He raised his arm and cupped her cheek in his palm. "Of course." Taking her elbow, he led her off the dance floor toward their table. "We'll leave right away."

A dark, raging storm had blown up the North Carolina coast by early Monday morning. Meghan could hear the wind howling outdoors and the large raindrops pelting the window pane of her grandmother's bedroom as she helped Deanna bathe and dress Hilary. She jumped at a loud knock on the door.

Sarah burst into the room, and Meghan stared in surprise at her sister's pale face and obvious distress.

"What is it?" She tried to keep her voice sounding as normal as possible, although it was more raspy and hoarse than ever. Since eating with Geoffrey the previous night, her headache had subsided considerably, but her throat was still raw.

Sarah stared back at her. "Meghan, what's wrong with you? You sound just awful."

"It's nothing. A little throat irritation."

"Are you sure? Let me look at you." She grasped Meghan's shoulders and leaned toward her until their noses were inches from each other. "You look terrible too. Tell me what's wrong."

Meghan forced a reassuring smile and tried to make her voice express a cheerfulness she was far from feeling. "Sarah, honey, you're the one who rushed in here all upset. What is it?"

Her sister nodded. "It's the horrible weather. Have you been listening to the reports?"

"Yes, it sounds quite miserable out there," Deanna said.

"No, I mean the forecast. The radio has been recommending voluntary evacuation of Hatteras Island. I guess local authorities are concerned the tropical storm will be coming right up the coast at us here."

"Soon?" Meghan's mind raced with concern and mental preparations.

"By this afternoon. Most of my friends have already packed and are ready to head inland, even though we were planning to have a long weekend stay because the Fourth fell on Sunday this year."

Giving Meghan a worried glance, Deanna began to fill a nylon bag with soaps, lotions, and medications. "I'll pack Hilary's essential personal and medical items and be ready to leave in five minutes."

Meghan nodded and turned to Sarah. "Are you able to go with Grandma? I'll stay here and see that the rest of the guests and household staff get off safely, and then I'll close up the house."

Sarah chewed her bottom lip. "But what if you get caught in this storm?"

"I'll be okay, Sarah. I'd like you to help Deanna with Grandma."

Meghan wrapped her arms around the younger woman's shoulders and gave her a gentle squeeze. "I won't get caught. I'll be careful, I promise. Go with Grandma and Deanna so I can be sure you all get inland ahead of the storm."

She brushed strands of hair from Sarah's face. "What about Zach and Geoffrey? Do they know about the evacuation?"

"They're packing their car now."

* * *

Geoffrey answered the telephone on the first ring. When he heard his mother's greeting on the other end of the line, he tossed his swimming towel in a nearby chair and sat down on the edge of the bed.

"I wasn't sure if I'd catch you in, my dear. How was your weekend at the beach?"

"Memorable." Elusive brown eyes, an unforgettable floral scent, and the musical sound of unexpected laughter filled his mind with intense tenacity. Meghan Blake had not left his thoughts for a second since he had held her in his arms on the tiny dance floor of the island restaurant the previous night.

"I hope that means that you and Zach are still speaking to each other."

"Yes, we're fine. I'm sure you'll be happy to know that I've had a change of heart."

"Oh?" Amanda Wright's voice rose in question over the telephone line.

"I made a public announcement at their engagement party and have given them my full support. He loves Sarah, Mother. There's no denying it. I'll have no peace if I continue to fight him over this marriage issue. Get ready for an autumn wedding."

"How wonderful! Now, what about you, Geoff? You met no beauties on the beach who caught your eye or stole your heart?"

Only the one with brown eyes and an unstoppable drive to work, a beauty with creamy smooth shoulders and curly thick lashes that fluttered in nervous motions whenever I made an attempt to distract her. "No, Mother, there was not one beach beauty in sight all weekend."

Amanda laughed. "That's a shame, my dear; but I will not give up my dream of having more grandchildren."

"Dream away, Mother." He wished she would not bring

up the same uncomfortable topic every time she called. "By the way, I have a question that is completely off the subject of matrimony and grandchildren. Do you know if Dad ever considered selling Wright Pharmaceuticals?"

"Why, no, I don't think so. Your father had a special interest in that particular part of the company. He established Wright Pharmaceuticals with his brother just a few years before your Uncle Zachary died. They were going to build it up together and develop it into an innovative medical research firm. As I remember, your father and uncle had outlined specific plans for it that were to be carried out even in the event of their deaths."

"Especially drug research, right?"

"Yes, they had the vision of developing drugs that would enhance the quality of life for people with debilitating diseases. Of course, their ultimate goal was to find cures, and your father and Zachary recruited some of the best specialists in the country to join Wright Pharmaceuticals with that goal in mind."

"I remember giving presentations with Dad to students with business and medical majors. At the time, ten years ago, the company was making rapid developments in the treatment of Cystic Fibrosis."

"That's right. At first, Cystic Fibrosis was its main emphasis."

"But hasn't Wright Pharmaceuticals made some recent breakthroughs in neurological research?"

"In the past few years, the main focus has been on the development of drugs to relieve the symptoms of Alzheimer's disease."

Amanda's answer did not surprise him, and he was silent as he allowed himself a few minutes of speculation on the whole subject. His attention was pulled back to the telephone by the sound of his mother's voice.

"Geoffrey? Are you there? Is something wrong?"

"No, no, Mother. Everything is fine. I think I'm going to have someone at Wright Pharmaceuticals fax me some statistics on current research projects. The offices are closed today. Aren't you personal friends with the director of research and development there?"

"Yes, Rob Benway has headed that department for about six years now. Let me check my address book for his home number."

Soon after Amanda gave Geoffrey the information he requested, she ended the conversation. Geoffrey found himself whistling as he picked up his towel and headed for the hotel pool.

"What's all this?" Zach strode across the large room between the bedrooms in their hotel suite a few hours later. "You look busy."

Geoffrey glanced up from his seat on the sofa in front of a low table scattered with papers. "I'm doing a little research."

His nephew dropped into an adjacent chair and leaned toward him to read the headings of several of the reports. "The family pharmaceutical company? Is something interesting happening?"

Geoffrey smiled. "Some incredible research, actually."

Zach pick up one of the papers. "It looks like Wright Pharmaceuticals is doing some fantastic work in new drug studies. Are these statistics accurate?"

"As far as I can tell. Here's an article from the *New England Journal of Medicine* about one particular project that has been tracking the effects of a synthetic enzyme on the symptoms of Alzheimer's disease. Early results indicate that progressive memory loss has been slowed and, in some cases, reversed slightly."

Zach stared at him. "Have you been doing this all afternoon?"

"Most of it. Why?"

"I just hope you haven't caught some of Sarah's sister's unhealthy work habits."

"You don't need to worry about that. I find too much pleasure in relaxing and having fun. I have a full week of meetings starting Monday, and then I have to fly to Atlanta to attend a regional medical supply conference. After that, I'm heading out to Cape Cod for the remainder of the summer."

Geoffrey leaned back against the sofa. "What are your plans?"

"I'm driving down to the Blake house for dinner in a little while. We were going to eat here in town, but I don't like the idea of Sarah having to get out in this weather. Would you like to join us?"

"Thanks, but I think I'll stick around here this evening." Geoffrey began to stack the papers together in organized piles. "Do you know if Meghan is working at her office today?"

"I'm sure she is, although Sarah tried her hardest to convince her sister to stay at home after Meghan's terrible drive back from Hatteras this morning." He studied Geoffrey. "Why?"

"I thought I might give her a call."

"Your interest in Meghan seems to involve more than simple courtesy toward my fiancée's family, Geoff. Do you like her?"

He sighed. "I don't know how I feel about her, to be quite honest. Her professional drive frustrates, as well as fascinates, me. Her constant need to be in control of her environment and her emotions is extremely baffling at times and, I might add, she doesn't care much for me."

"How do you know that?"

For a moment, Geoffrey considered telling Zach about

Meghan's offer to buy Wright Pharmaceuticals. "I think I make her uncomfortable. She can't seem to relax with me."

"Meghan's that way with everyone. She's so uptight that she makes me agitated whenever I'm around her. She's a brilliant business executive but very much lacking in skills as a member of a family."

Geoffrey nodded. "She had that same nervous drive even as a young student at Harvard."

Zach looked surprised. "I didn't know you knew her then."

"Not knew, exactly, but we met one evening when I gave my annual presentation on the Wright Company to students pursuing business majors."

"The same colloquium where Sarah and I met? Isn't that interesting?"

"Yes, almost eerie." Geoffrey did not want to mention his suspicions regarding Meghan's sister and his nephew's *chance* meeting. "Anyway, Meghan bombarded me with questions. She wanted to know everything there was to know about business. I had a hard time keeping up with her quest for knowledge regarding commercial enterprise."

"And just look at what she's accomplished in the business world. Who knows, Geoff? Maybe you were a major influence on the success of her career."

"I would rather be a major influence on her success as a sister. Her deteriorating relationship with Sarah bothers me. It's probably none of my business, but I've grown rather fond of your fiancée and I don't want to see her hurt."

"Sarah is beginning to like you too. She doesn't even call you an old man anymore. You really impressed her with your skills at the pool table."

Zach sighed. "Meghan, though, could certainly develop a few skills in being a sister. Sarah mostly just wants Meghan to spend some time with her—you know, talking, watching old movies, shopping. She wants to do the kinds of things sisters typically do together, like when Grandma and her sisters get together."

Geoffrey nodded. "I know, and it's very sad to see her trying so hard to get Meghan's attention. It's a wonder Sarah hasn't stopped trying after all these years."

"I love Sarah, Geoff, but I know she misses her sister and needs Meghan's love too."

Geoffrey met Meghan at a small, casual riverfront restaurant just a few blocks from the main headquarters of Blake Industries. He had been surprised, as well as delighted, when she called and invited him to her office Monday evening.

Since he had not yet eaten, and was sure that she had not, also, he suggested that they meet for dinner. Consistent with the typical behavior with which he was growing accustomed, she had, of course, insisted she had too much to do to take time for a meal; but in the end his persistence wore her down, and she agreed to join him.

As he gazed at her from across the table, he thought her face looked thin and drawn. "How was your drive from the Outer Banks?"

Their server set glasses of lemonade and pieces of crusty bread with a bowl of spinach and cheese dip in front of them. In the flickering light of a hurricane lantern, he watched her wince as she sipped the cold drink.

"Terrible. I fought the wind and rain all the way."

"That's certainly some storm. Zach said Sarah and your grandmother and her nurse had no problems getting back."

"No, thank goodness. I worried about them the whole drive back."

He did not recognize the usually strong, persuasive voice that had attempted to convince him, just a few days ago, to sell his family's pharmaceutical firm. Her appearance alarmed him. Dark circles under her eyes and sunken cheek bones were signs of extreme fatigue.

"When I called from the office, Sarah said that, except for the heavy rain, the trip was uneventful for them."

He watched her play with a piece of bread on her plate. "You've been working all day?"

She raised tired brown eyes and met his gaze. "I was able to catch up on a tremendous amount of work without interruptions because the offices were actually closed for the holiday."

When their broiled lemon chicken and asparagus arrived, he watched a pained expression mask her face as she attempted to swallow a bite of food. Picking up his own fork, he speared a stalk of the crisp vegetable on his plate. "I must say, Meghan, that I was intrigued by your invitation to meet this evening. Am I to assume that tonight's dinner is not a simple social one?"

She set her fork down and looked at him with eyes that had definitely lost some of their usual luster and alertness. She appeared to consider her words with care before she spoke. "All day, I've been reviewing my proposal regarding Wright Pharmaceuticals."

"Oh?" He waited with patience he was far from feeling.

She inhaled a long, deep breath. "After much thought on the matter, I have reconsidered my initial plan to purchase your firm."

Reconsidered? Her announcement could not have been more shocking if it had been accompanied by a burst of Independence Day fireworks. He took a steady breath to calm his nerves. "You're withdrawing your proposal, just like that?"

She nodded as she traced the rim of her glass with her fingertips. Did he detect a tremor in them? "It's for the best, I believe, at least for the time being."

He leaned back in his chair and leveled his eyes on her. "I admit that you've caught me by complete surprise. I thought I had discovered the reason for your adamant pursuit of Wright Pharmaceuticals this past year. You've been following the progress the research and development department has been making in Alzheimer's studies. This has been a crusade for your grandmother."

A shadow crossed her pale face. Of what? Regret? Resignation? She was so quiet. Where was the vibrant, eager business woman who emanated confidence and power with every action?

"You must know, then, that you're doing the most innovative work in Alzheimer's research in the whole country. Your advances in treating the symptoms of the disease are phenomenal, to say the least."

"And you're no longer concerned with profits?"

"As you well know, financial gain is important in any business endeavor. The Wright Company as a whole has flourished under your leadership, Geoffrey." She sighed. "I still believe that with the proper management, Wright Pharmaceuticals itself could become the thriving, lucrative enterprise your family once envisioned it to be."

He reached for his lemonade. "Then why the change in position? You haven't given up your enthusiasm and hope in finding a cure for Alzheimer's?"

"No, of course not. I just think it would be better for Sarah and Zach if I discontinued my pursuit of any kind of merger at this time."

"Sarah and Zach?"

"I don't want anyone, including the public, in general, to think that this marriage has anything to do with a plot to combine Blake Industries and the Wright Company."

He breathed a long sigh of relief. "No old fashioned plan of a 'marriage of convenience,' then?"

He thought he noticed a hint of a smile on her pale lips. "I'm afraid that Sarah and Zach are going to have a hard enough time as it is with all of their romantic ideals and unrealistic dreams, but I certainly do not want any decisions I make in the name of Blake Industries to jeopardize their chances of a successful marriage."

Fighting the urge to rise from his seat and take her in his arms, he leaned across the table and reached for her hand. "So, you've accepted the fact that our charges are going to make one of the most important commitments of their young lives? You're promising to lend them your support?"

"Nothing so magnanimous as that, I'm afraid." She caught her lower lip between her teeth, a behavior he had seen Sarah exhibit when the younger woman was troubled. "I still have nagging doubts that Sarah is making a big mistake. My father married three times, Geoffrey. Each one brought him heartache and disappointment. He died at forty-eight, bitter, disillusioned, and alone. His three wives had divorced him. His only son had died, and the only comfort in his life had been his work. I can't help thinking that Sarah is destined to experience that kind of pain and sadness."

He locked his fingers with hers. "Zach is not your father, Meghan. His parents were happily married for fifteen years until they were killed in an automobile accident. My parents had a joyous marriage for twenty-five years. Not all unions end in divorce. Weren't your grandparents happy?" He held her gaze as he watched her smile. Was she remembering Hilary and her grandfather during a special moment? "See? Couples make their own happiness. Life doesn't have to be full of disappointment and sadness."

He reached out and traced her trembling chin with his fingertips. "At one time, I experienced a similar period of disillusionment regarding love and romance. Events happen in our lives that hurt and confuse us so much that we decide to bury the memories inside us because we think that denying them will save us from getting hurt again. I've come to realize that refusing to recognize and deal with the memories doesn't really do anything, though, but keep us isolated and unhappy."

He felt her fingers tighten in his hand as tears slid down her pale cheeks. Closing her eyes, she pulled away from his grasp. "I should be getting back to the office."

Geoffrey tried to calm his racing heartbeat. He wanted to hold her and protect her and care for her. Why? She did not need him—that fact was clear.

Chapter Seven

Over two weeks later, Geoffrey was still trying to get Meghan Blake off his mind. Why was he having such a difficult time forgetting her? He snapped his suitcase shut as a knock on the hotel door interrupted his silent reflections.

"All set?" Zach strode toward the bed. "I'm glad you stopped here on your way back from Atlanta, but I wish you didn't have to leave again so soon."

"You're welcome to come with me." Geoffrey began stacking budget reports into a manageable pile.

"No way! From now on, when there's a choice between you and Sarah, I'm going to choose spending time with her. Being in love is such a great feeling!" His nephew watched him collect papers. "I understand you had dinner with Meghan again before you left for Boston. You like her, don't you? There's no point in denying it, Geoff. I can see it. My cynical, lifelong bachelor uncle is having a hard time resisting the overwhelming power of love."

"I am certainly not in love with Meghan Blake."

"Are you sure?" Zach smiled. "If I'm right, you have my sympathies. You'll have your hands full trying to develop a satisfying relationship with such an independent worka-holic. I've had absolutely no luck getting to know her."

"I have no plans to involve myself in any kind of relation-ship with Meghan, other than keeping on good terms with her as your future sister-in-law. At this point, I believe she is, at least, warming up to the idea of your marriage to Sarah."

"Yes. What's the sudden change in attitude about, any-way? Sarah was actually able to discuss some tentative wed-ding plans with her last night. Now Sarah's worried some business dilemma will develop at the last minute, and Meghan will miss the ceremony."

Geoffrey chuckled. "Tell Sarah she has to be patient with her sister's newfound acceptance. This is a big step for Meghan. I think you were right when you suggested she uses work to distract herself from her fears and feelings."

"Maybe you're the one to help Meghan finally open up a bit and take a few emotional risks. She seems to give you more time and attention than she gives anyone else." Zach watched as he collected another pile of reports. "Are you still studying those Wright Pharmaceutical reports?"

"Just trying to keep up with new developments. Do you think you'll ever be interested in heading the family business someday?"

"Business is hardly my thing, but I have been considering getting involved in some public relations work. I could use what I've learned in my photography and journalism classes to work for almost any kind of organization. In fact, the career development office at school's found several prospective posi-tions for me to look at, right here in the Hampton Roads area."

"What about your job with that agency in Cambridge? Weren't you planning to take wedding pictures and family portraits this summer?"

"Before I left to come down here, I warned the head photographer that I was thinking about staying in Virginia for awhile. I've found a little apartment in Portsmouth."

"Oh?" Geoffrey slid his arms into the sleeves of his suit jacket and placed his wallet and airline ticket in the inside pocket.

"Sarah wants to be here, close to her family, especially since her grandmother's condition is so unstable. Boston is a long way from Newport News and the Blake estate."

"Does Sarah have a job?"

"She's thinking about taking a part-time position at Blake Industries."

"Really?"

"She figures she'll get to spend more time with Meghan if they're working together."

Geoffrey smiled. "Then it would be a lot harder for Meghan to ignore her, you mean?"

Zach nodded. "There's a temporary opening in the public relations department at Blake Industries, and they're looking for people to redesign and update brochures for their educational division."

Geoffrey was not sure he understood. "You're not considering working there, are you?"

His nephew's gaze was steady. "Not if you'd have objections."

"No, of course not."

"I wouldn't be showing disloyalty to the Wright Company?"

Geoffrey reached out and squeezed Zach's shoulder. "I believe I've finally learned my lesson about interfering in your life. At least, your grandmother says I have."

The younger man grinned. "I don't even know if Meghan will okay it. She has the final say on everyone who gets hired at Blake Industries, and I'm not sure she likes me that much."

Geoffrey chuckled. "Sometimes I wonder if your future sister-in-law likes anyone, really. On the other hand, your skills are exemplary; and you are dependable and responsible. She is an astute employer and not likely to pass up a valuable asset to her company because of a personal bias."

"Well, whether or not Meghan hires me, I'll find a job of some sort. I want to be ready to provide for Sarah's financial, as well as emotional, needs. Even if I'm not able to afford the lifestyle she's used to, I'm going to give her a comfortable home without having to use money from our personal trust funds. We'd like to invest that money in accounts reserved for our children's education."

"You have been doing some planning. What about your dream to help people in South America?"

"We haven't given up on that idea completely; but right now, Sarah wants to stay close to home and to her grandmother. She's been more worried than usual about Hilary's health."

"So has Meghan, although she goes to great lengths not to admit it."

Zach rose to his feet. "You're certainly noticing a lot about Meghan, while insisting you are a disinterested observer." He grinned again. "You like her, don't you? Why are you so reluctant to admit it? Are you ashamed of your feelings?"

Geoffrey avoided his nephew's eyes. "I'm not ashamed of my feelings. Meghan Blake and I have absolutely nothing in common, and I don't mind telling you that this whole topic of conversation is making me extremely uncomfortable." Geoffrey headed toward the door. "Isn't Sarah joining us this morning?"

Zach nodded. "She's meeting us in the hotel dining room. She was stopping by Meghan's office to set up a time to go shopping for bridesmaids' dresses."

Although the hotel dining room was busy, they waited only

a few minutes before they were shown to a table. "Let's go ahead and order, Geoff. Sarah should be here any minute."

Geoffrey was still reading the breakfast menu when Zach rose to his feet. "There she is. She looks upset." Zach took her hand and guided the young woman to a chair between them. "What's up, sweetheart?"

"Oh, Zach, after my talk with Meghan last night, I thought we'd made some progress. I thought she'd finally begun to change." After gulping a large drink of water from her glass, she flipped a strand of hair over one of her shoulders. "I went to her office, but she wasn't there. She couldn't even bother to wait before running off to a meeting."

Zach squeezed her hand. "Some important business probably popped up. She didn't leave you a message?"

Sarah shook her head. "I forgot and left my pager and phone at home, but her secretary said she rushed out without warning or explanation. My name was the only one in her appointment book until nine o'clock."

Something in the young woman's response disturbed Geoffrey. "That's odd, isn't it, Sarah? I thought that Meghan was always very meticulous about recording her appointments."

Sarah shrugged and picked up a menu. "Usually, I suppose. What are you thinking?"

"Nothing, I guess. Let's eat."

The conversation turned to lighter subjects as their breakfast arrived. Zach and Sarah talked about plans to visit some historical sights and a local theme park. Geoffrey discussed his plans to relax at the Wright family's summer home on Cape Cod.

A server approached their table. "Excuse me, sir. Are you Geoffrey Wright? You have an urgent call."

Urgent? Geoffrey reached for the telephone the server

handed him as anxious thoughts raced through his mind.
"Geoffrey. I'm glad I caught you. It's Meghan."

Her voice was so hoarse and low that she was barely audible. He knew in an instant that something was wrong.

"Is Sarah there at the hotel with you? I've been trying to reach her, but she's not answering her phone or pager."

"Meghan, slow down. Yes, Sarah's here. Tell me what's happened."

He heard her sob. "It's Grandma. She's had another stroke. Will you tell Sarah to come to the hospital right away?"

Before he could answer, she hung up. Zach and Sarah stared at him as he turned back toward them.

Sarah's lips were trembling. "It's bad news, isn't it?"

Geoffrey nodded. "Your grandmother has been taken to the hospital. Meghan wants you to meet her there."

Zach slipped his arm around her shaking shoulders as tears streamed down her cheeks. "I'll take you, sweetheart."

Nodding, she turned to Geoffrey. "Will you come, too?"

The small waiting room was nearly deserted as Geoffrey sat in a wooden chair and browsed through a current news magazine. Uncrossing his legs, he glanced at his watch. It had been over two hours since Sarah and Zach had been escorted by a solemn faced nurse to Hilary Blake's private room, and Geoffrey had been directed to a waiting room down the hall. Although many seats began to fill with anxious relatives and friends of other patients in that wing, it was nearly noon before Zach and Sarah returned. Geoffrey rose from his chair as Zach guided his fiancée to a seat next to him, where the young woman slumped and covered her face with her hands.

After a few moments, Sarah looked up and gave Geoffrey a weak smile. "Thank you for being here, Geoff. Having you and Zach near is such a comfort."

He reached out and patted her shoulder. "How is your grandmother doing?"

"Not good, I'm afraid." Tears brimmed her green eyes. "Her heart has stopped twice since she was brought in. The hospital staff had to resuscitate her and defibrillate her heart. Now she's on a respirator and not responding to anyone or anything."

As she burst into tears, Zach rushed to put his arms around her. "I think we both need a little break, sweetheart. Let's take a walk. We could get a drink, or something to eat in the cafeteria."

Sarah shook her head. "We've already been gone too long. Deanna went to check on those test results, and Meghan is all alone with Grandma."

Over Sarah's auburn head, Zach met his uncle's eyes. "Would you mind going to sit with Meghan in Hilary's room for a short time, Geoff, while we go get something to drink? I think Sarah needs to clear her head. We won't be long."

Following Zach's directions, Geoffrey found the room without a problem. As he stepped into the dimness, he focused first on the elderly woman in the bed connected to various monitors and intravenous tubes. When his eyes adjusted to the lack of light, he saw Meghan leaning forward in a metal chair as she held one of Hilary's thin hands.

As he walked toward her, Meghan lifted her pale tear dampened face and gave him a faint smile. "Geoffrey, I didn't know you were here."

"I came to keep you company for a few minutes while Zach and Sarah get some fresh air."

She wiped her eyes with a wadded tissue. "My sister isn't taking this very well."

"She's scared and worried."

"We knew it was likely to happen again. When Grandma

suffered the first stroke, the doctors told us she would probably have another one."

"That knowledge probably doesn't offer much consolation to either one of you right now."

"No, it doesn't."

Geoffrey listened to the rhythmic sound of the respirator. It was obvious that Meghan was keeping a tight reign on her feelings. He approached her chair and set a light hand on her shoulder.

"She's so tiny and frail." Meghan's voice was low and raspy. "She's just a shell of the person she used to be. My grandmother was always so vibrant and full of life."

As he stood looking at Hilary, he could only imagine her as a healthy, productive human being. He supposed that she could have been a combination of the lighthearted, idealistic Sarah and the serious, intellectual Meghan. Perhaps that was the reason the two sisters were so different. They may have inherited opposite extremes of Hilary's personality. His heart was heavy at the realization that he would never know her for who she really was.

Beneath his hand, he felt Meghan's shoulder tremble. A convulsive breath shook her body, and he drew her into his arms. "Go ahead and cry, Meghan. I'm right here." Feeling helpless and ineffective, he simply held her as she wept.

When the door of Hilary's room swung open, Meghan pulled away from him and wiped her eyes with a tissue. He glanced at Deanna Fuller as she entered.

Meghan inhaled a deep breath. "Are the test results back?"

The private nurse nodded. "Dr. Elliston would like to see you and your sister in his office immediately."

"Sarah's not here." Meghan turned to Geoffrey.

He welcomed the opportunity to be useful in some way. "I'll go find her."

Zach and Sarah were seated at a corner table away from

the busy lunch crowd when he entered the bustling cafeteria. Zach had his arm draped around Sarah's shoulder, and their heads were bowed together in conversation. He saw the young woman smile, and he was glad that his nephew was able to provide a moment of cheer amid her distress.

As he approached their table, Sarah looked up with sad, hazel eyes. "The test results are back?"

He nodded. "The doctor is waiting to talk with you."

She pressed her lips together as Zach kissed her cheek. "Hold on, sweetheart."

As Geoffrey followed the young couple from the cafeteria, he could not help wondering what tests had been done and if the results would determine Hilary Blake's prognosis. Both Meghan and Sarah appeared anxious about what the doctor would say to them.

While the two Blake sisters hurried together to another wing of the hospital, Hilary's private nurse stayed with their grandmother. Zach accompanied Geoffrey back to the waiting room where he had spent most of the morning. They found two empty seats near a window overlooking a small courtyard blooming with brilliant summer flowers and lush green shrubbery. Taking off his suit jacket and draping it over the back of an adjacent chair, Geoffrey studied a bed of yellow and orange day lilies before turning to face his nephew.

Zach stopped flipping through the magazine in his hands and met his eyes. "I think the doctor's going to tell them that there's really no hope. The respirator is keeping their grandmother alive."

Geoffrey was silent as he forced himself to make sense of Zach's words. "There's no chance that she will recover?"

Zach shook his head. "I don't think so. The last stroke did too much damage."

"Do Sarah and Meghan realize the extent of the damage?"

"They do. Sarah, I think, has begun to accept what's inevitable and is preparing herself for her grandmother's death."

"And Meghan?"

"She's still denying it."

Geoffrey sighed. "I feel so helpless. She's trying to be strong. She doesn't want to show anyone how vulnerable she really is."

Zach nodded as he set the magazine back on a nearby table. "She's going to fall hard when the reality finally hits her. She pushes everyone away. I don't think Meghan's prepared to handle her grief all alone."

Geoffrey turned back to gaze at the flowers outside the window. "She's keeping her true feelings inside and hidden, even from those who care about her."

Zach rose and set his hand on Geoffrey's shoulder. "Meghan is not the only one denying feelings right now."

Chapter Eight

"I can't go, Meghan. I just can't." Sarah's hazel eyes glistened with unshed tears and a silent plea as she looked up at Meghan from her seat on the carpet in front of the living room fireplace. Photo albums and boxes of snapshots and newspaper clippings were scattered in a circle around her.

"Sarah, we have to be at the funeral home in a half an hour."

The younger woman shook her head, and her hair brushed against her trembling shoulders. "I wouldn't be any help at all. I'm an emotional wreck. All I want to do is cry."

Meghan pressed her fingers to her temples. The dull pain there had evolved into a constant pounding in a thick band around her head. The intense throbbing impeded her concentration every time she moved. She knew she was sick, but she did not have time to think about that complication in her life.

She watched Sarah turn the pages of an old photo album. "What are you looking at?"

Her sister sniffled. "Pictures of Grandma. Here she is dressed up for one of her cotillions. Come look."

Meghan swallowed. Her throat, still sore and swollen,

111

worried her. She could barely speak without revealing her discomfort to others, but the grief of her grandmother's death was even more painful.

Crossing the floor, she leaned over to see the picture to which Sarah pointed and nodded. "When she was sixteen. Wasn't she beautiful?"

"I love her gown, all white and silky and flowing. Look at all of those white lilies. The place must have been decorated with thousands of them."

Meghan smiled and smoothed Sarah's hair with her hand. "They were her favorite flowers."

"Oh, look at this one. Remember all of the picnics at the beach? Grandma always packed that big wicker basket so full that it took all three of us to carry it across the dunes."

"And everything still tasted delicious even when a breeze blew sand over our blanket." Meghan sat down beside Sarah on the floor. "Gritty sandwiches, gritty pickles, gritty cookies, but they always tasted better than any meal at home."

Sarah turned another page. "Here we are taking the ferry to Ocracoke Island. I remember how you'd try to sit on the railing right out in front, where you could feel the wind head-on, until Grandma made you get down. You were such a brat."

"You were the brat, you little snitch!" She gave her sister's ribs a gentle jab with her elbow. "She wouldn't have known I was up there if you hadn't always run to tattle to her."

Sarah smiled through her tears. "I was so afraid you'd fall in the water."

"Fall in what water?" Zach appeared in the doorway of the living room. "What's all this?"

"Remembrances of Grandma." Sarah beckoned to him. "Come join us." She held up a loose snap shot for Zach and Meghan to see. "A view from the top of the Cape Hatteras lighthouse, the day Meghan climbed it five times without stopping."

Zach's eyes widened in disbelief as he squatted beside his fiancée. "Five times?"

Meghan shrugged. "Sarah dared me to do it. She bet me her week's allowance that I couldn't. See, there she is at the bottom waving at me. I took the picture to commemorate my victory."

"You lost your allowance?" Zach took Sarah's hand in his. "Did you ever win a bet you made with Meghan?"

The younger woman shook her head. "Never."

"That's because your sister accepts any challenge with extraordinary earnestness. I've found she doesn't like to lose."

All three turned to see Geoffrey standing in the doorway. Meghan's heart thumped in her chest as she looked at him. In dark casual pants and a pressed oxford shirt, his presence instantly warmed her, despite the overwhelming sorrow that threatened her wavering composure and the illness that made her body feel weak and her mind unfocused.

Sarah rolled her eyes. "You can say that again. Meghan and losing—it'll just never happen. You should play rummy with her."

Geoffrey met Meghan's eyes. His own sparkled with apparent anticipation. "I look forward to it."

With difficulty, she pulled away her gaze and swallowed the lump that had formed in her swollen throat. She put her hand on Sarah's back and rubbed it. "It's time to make arrangements for Grandma's funeral, honey."

Her sister's hair veiled her face as she shook her head. "No, I can't, Meghan. Please don't make me."

Meghan brushed auburn strands from Sarah's face and kissed her forehead. "Are you sure?"

"I'm sure." As tears slid down her cheeks, Sarah forced a smile. "Just remember the white lilies, okay?"

For a moment, Meghan worried she would cry too. She watched Zach slip his arm around Sarah's waist.

"I'll stay with her while you're gone, Meghan."

Squeezing Zach's shoulder, Meghan rose to her feet and smoothed out the fabric of her dark skirt with the palms of her hands. She was glad her little sister had Zach to help her through this awful time of grief. He was so considerate and understanding. She knew now that she had been wrong to try to interfere with Sarah's plans to marry him. They were perfect for each other.

She felt a hand on her arm as she picked her way around the collection of pictures on the floor. She looked up into questioning gray eyes.

"Sarah's going to stay here. She's not feeling quite up to accompanying me this morning."

He set a gentle hand on her shoulder. "Are you? Up to it, I mean?"

With a sigh, she glanced at Sarah and Zach, still looking through old photos albums. "Not really, I guess, but one of us has to do it."

"I'll come with you."

In contrast to the rhythmic pounding in her head, Geoffrey's quiet baritone voice felt like a soft, comforting ocean breeze against her skin. She closed her eyes. "That's not necessary. I can do this."

He moved his hand to her cheek and rubbed it with his palm. "I'm not doubting your ability. I thought you might like the company."

Without thinking, she leaned against his hand and enjoyed its power to console her, if only for a moment. She was not at all sure she wanted to spend the morning with the one person who seemed to possess the capacity to unnerve her and fill her mind with unrealistic ideas and romantic thoughts. With reluctance, she opened her eyes and gave him a slight nod that sent a wave of pain piercing through her head. "If you're sure you don't mind—"

When he smiled, it felt like he was embracing her. She could imagine his strong, gentle arms holding and comforting her. The vivid musing made her heart skip a beat.

His kind gray eyes met hers. "Your car or mine?"

Despite her reservations regarding her acceptance of Geoffrey Wright's offer to accompany her, she had to admit that he was helpful and supportive without being overly protective or assertive. By lunch time, both the funeral service and burial arrangements had been made. Each step in the long, detailed process was a painful reminder of her beloved grandmother's passing, but Meghan pressed forward, trying with great difficulty not to break down and give into her tears.

"Blakes don't cry." She recalled her father's words the day her mother died. *"Hold your head high. No tears,"* he told her at her brother's funeral. *"Displaying emotion is to admit weakness. Sadness and regret serve no purpose in our lives. Pull yourself together and prove to the world that John Blake's daughter is stronger than any tragedy the world throws at her."*

As they crossed the parking lot of the church, Meghan glanced at her watch. The calling hours at the funeral home would begin at seven that evening. She would still have time to notify several people who may not have heard the news of her grandmother's death.

The remnants of the tropical storm at the end of the recent holiday weekend had passed over a week ago, and in its place had come an oppressive, humid heat. The hot, still air did little to clear her mind as she inhaled a slow breath. The act of squinting into the glare of the sun sent pain throbbing through her head. She stepped on a loose stone and lost her footing.

She would have fallen to the ground if Geoffrey had not reached out and caught her elbow. As she steadied herself, she tipped her head up to intense gray eyes filled with concern. With effort, she pulled her gaze away and fumbled in her shoulder bag for her keys. After several failed attempts, Geoffrey reached past her and located the ring of keys with his own hand. Aware of his undeniable presence, she watched him unlock the car with the remote control button. Trying to ignore the pounding in her head and the nausea in her stomach, she opened the door and sank into the seat. Her temples throbbed as she closed her eyes and leaned against the headrest. If she could just sit still for a few minutes, then perhaps the pain would ease off, allowing her to concentrate again. The gentle touch of his hand on her cheek sent a wave of warmth through her, and she forced her eyes to open.

"Are you sick, Meghan?"

"I don't have time to be sick."

He moved his hand down to lift her chin with his fingertips until their eyes met. "Life doesn't always unfold into a nice convenient schedule. Other than following a healthy lifestyle, we don't usually have a choice of when or where we get sick."

She tried to pull her gaze away from him, but his intense eyes held her in an inexplicable bond as heat radiated from his touch.

"I think you're running a fever."

She shook her head. "It's hot in here. Give me my keys so I can start the air conditioning."

"Slide over."

"What?"

"I'm going to drive."

"I'm fine, Geoffrey."

"You're sick."

"I'm not."

"You are. You've had a headache and a sore throat for days, and now you have a fever. You may be able to deceive others, my dear, but I can see right through that invincible shield of yours."

When she began to protest, he narrowed his eyes at her. "If you force my hand, Meghan, I'll just pick you up and move you. Now, scoot over."

She studied the resolve in his handsome face and realized that arguing with him would serve no purpose. His determination was exceptional. Without another word, she moved to the passenger seat. Despite her initial objections, she found she was grateful to relinquish the responsibility of driving back home. Her head hurt too much to focus on the road.

Sarah met them at the front door as Meghan and Geoffrey climbed the wide, marble steps into the pillared, three-story structure overlooking Virginia's Chesapeake Bay. The scent of fresh flowers took Meghan's breath away as they stepped into the foyer, where huge floral arrangements in ceramic pots and crystal vases lined all four walls.

After giving her a hug, Sarah threw up her arms. "Flowers keep arriving. I've started sending the delivery vans right to the funeral home. We're running out of room here. The phone's been ringing constantly. Were you able to get everything arranged at the funeral home and church?"

"Everything's set. We have to be back at the funeral home by six-thirty tonight."

Her sister reached out and squeezed her hand. "I'm sorry about this morning. I just needed some time to collect myself. I guess I needed some hugs too—Zach's really good at giving those." Sarah turned to Geoffrey. "It was wonderful of you to help out, Geoff. Let's go eat. Zach has lunch set up on the back verandah."

Meghan glanced at her watch. "I'd better not take the time. I have to make some calls."

Sarah stared at Meghan. "You sound terrible, Meghan,

and you look terrible too. Are you sure you shouldn't eat something? Oh, I almost forgot—on your desk in your study, I put a list of people who would like you to call when you have time. Several individuals want to make memorial donations to the Blake Family Foundation in Grandma's name, and they want details about the Alzheimer's Walk for a Cure that we sponsor in June. Oh, and some secretaries from your office telephoned numerous times before Carly called to apologize for the disruptions. They won't be bothering you anymore today."

"The office? I'd better see what's going on."

"No, Carly said everything was fine."

"Go ahead and start lunch without me. I'll be in my study."

Sitting at her desk minutes later, Meghan stole a moment to rest her head before attacking the long list of tasks she needed to complete in the next few hours. The pounding at her temples made concentrating difficult.

She straightened in her chair at the sound of approaching footsteps. The appearance of Geoffrey Wright no longer surprised her, but he still managed to elicit from her an inexplicable sense of contentedness.

"If you can't take time for lunch, I'll bring it to you."

He dismissed the shake of her head and set a tray in from of her. "Toast, melon, tea. Light, easy on the throat, and perfect for the woman who thinks she has too much to do."

His playful tone made her smile. "My list gets longer by the minute."

"You don't have to do it all by yourself, Meghan. Let me help."

She caught her lower lip between her teeth as it began to tremble. There he was, being kind and considerate to her again. Tears stung her eyes and threatened to fall. "How?"

He held out his hand. "Give me your list. Tell me what

tasks absolutely have to be done by you personally. Now, be honest. You're only one person, and no one expects you to do everything yourself, especially at a time like this."

"I need to call some of Grandma's close friends who live far away and may not have heard about her death. I need to check with Carly to finalize the agenda for the board meeting next week."

"Good. After you eat, make your calls in here on this phone line." He studied her list. "As soon as I eat, I'll call the people who have requested details about making memorial donations and participating in the Alzheimer's Walk for a Cure. I'll assign Zach the job of renting and supervising the arrangement of the tables and chairs for the luncheon after the funeral. I'll have Sarah take care of the coordination between your kitchen staff and the caterer. Anything else?"

She was amazed at the sense of relief that flooded over her just by sharing her responsibilities with him. "No, not that I can think of. Thank you, Geoff."

He smiled. "My pleasure, my dear. Now, enjoy that tea. I made it myself."

The next two days passed for Meghan in a fog of quiet shock, tightly controlled emotions, and relentless pain in her head and throat. A huge number of mourners arrived to pay their last respects to her grandmother who, before her illness, had been the wife of a prominent Virginia businessman, an active member of several charitable organizations and a well respected woman of high class southern society.

At the funeral home, Meghan stood for hours to greet and to offer words of solace to Hilary's old and dear friends. At the memorial service, she joined Sarah in speaking of their grandmother's life achievements, despite Meghan's failing voice. Throughout the solemn events, she sensed her body growing weaker and weaker.

At the cemetery Friday afternoon, she fought her own rising temperature as the air temperature soared. She found the heaviness of the humidity almost unbearable as she and Sarah placed bouquets of white lilies on the polished steel casket at the conclusion of the grave site service. Pressing her palms against the smooth metal, Meghan closed her eyes and said a last, silent good-bye to the woman who had been both mentor and friend to her. As she remembered her grandmother at the base of the Cape Hatteras lighthouse painting at her easel, she heard Sarah's quiet sobs and the muffled sounds of people leaving the Blake family mausoleum and driving away in their cars.

"The limousine is waiting for us whenever you're ready." Zach's voice reached her ears as he touched her shoulder. "I'm going to walk over there with Sarah. Take all the time you need."

She nodded, her eyes still closed to the sad scene around her. She imagined that her grandmother was now in a wonderfully peaceful place where her legs were no longer crippled, her memory no longer absent, and her thoughts no longer confused and unfocused. She would be beautiful again with thick auburn hair, blended with strands of brown and reds, like Sarah's, and bright blue expressive eyes and a warm happy smile.

Meghan fingered the soft, satin petal of a lily as she allowed her grandmother's animated face to drift across her mind one more time. She took a slow breath, but the damp still air seemed to stick to her lungs. She felt hot and tired as she opened her eyes. The casket seemed to sway before her, and her temples throbbed in pain. Her legs felt weak and rubbery as she stumbled backwards trying to steady herself.

"Careful there."

In an instant, Geoffrey's strong arms held her. "Easy, Meghan. I have you."

Keeping one arm in a firm hold around her waist, he used his free hand to touch her grandmother's casket. "She's at peace now, probably playing her own volleyball game on a beach somewhere with a bunch of noisy college students."

In spite of her spinning head and unstable legs, Meghan could not help but smile. "Grandma always had a killer serve."

His eyes looked down at her as a hint of a smile tugged at the corner of his mouth. "If you need more time here, I'll get you a chair."

"I just want a few more minutes." She rested her head on his arm. "I can't believe I'll never see her again."

Chapter Nine

"Oh, will you look at that. My worm's gone again, and I still haven't caught a single fish."

Geoffrey looked up from his book to see Sarah reel in an empty hook dangling from the end of her fishing line. With a grin, he shook his head.

Zach grimaced. "The only thing I've caught is weeds."

Geoffrey chuckled. The hot, humid day had cooled to a pleasant temperature, and he was enjoying the refreshing breeze that blew across the cove as he lounged in a lawn chair near the dock at the Blakes' estate on Chesapeake Bay. "It's a good thing we didn't count on you two to catch dinner tonight."

"I don't see you hauling any big catch in, Uncle." Zach threw him a playful grin. "Don't you know how to entice the little creatures onto the line?"

"I never rely on my inept angling skills to provide my meals. I always make sure I have plenty of food whenever I return from fishing."

"Hey, here comes Meghan." Sarah cast her line out into the water. "Come and join us!"

Geoffrey tossed the petite brunette a smile as she walked toward the sheltered cove of Chesapeake Bay. Since her grandmother's funeral, Meghan had stayed in her study or her bedroom, and he had not seen her. Now, in sandals and a lavender sun dress, she appeared more attractive than he had ever seen her—despite her drawn expression and dark circles under her eyes.

She took a seat in the chair next to his and watched Sarah and Zach on the dock. "How's the fishing going?"

"Not so well. You'll have to get out there and show those two amateurs how to do it. Sarah tells me you've been very successful at deep sea fishing."

"I haven't touched a pole in years, but I used to fish for hours from that dock."

He thought her voice held a wistful tone. Did she miss those carefree days? "Does anyone ever swim in the cove?"

"We did when we were younger. Sarah still does sometimes."

"Not you?"

"No, not anymore."

He studied the shadow that crossed her face as she waved to her sister and Zach. "Weren't you wearing a swim suit in the photograph on your desk at the beach house?"

She shifted in her chair and avoided his eyes. "That was a long time ago."

"You speak as though you're a hundred years old, my dear."

"Sometimes I feel a hundred years old."

"Why, Meghan? What makes you feel so old? Perhaps you were expected to mature too quickly and missed an essential part of your youth?"

With the pad of his thumb, he traced tiny, slow circles on the back of her hand. Breathing in her fresh scent of floral cologne, he began to feel lightheaded. Being near her was intoxicating.

"When I was eleven, my father insisted that I grow up.

After my brother died, he immediately began to prepare me for the role he had always envisioned his only son would play in the continued development of Blake Industries. Everything I did from that moment on was directed at honing my skills as a prospective and successful member of the business world. There were no more toys or games or playing with my friends. I was expected to work harder, study longer and perform better than any of my classmates in school. The only reprieve I ever had was when Grandma took Sarah and me to the Outer Banks. The rest of the time, I was expected to get ready to follow in my father's steps."

Geoffrey's heart was heavy as he listened to her describe the sad condition of her childhood. "And you always did what he wanted?"

She glanced at her sister on the dock. "I didn't mind. When my father was busy with me, he left Sarah alone. She got to keep her dolls and games and books of fairy tales."

Geoffrey shook his head. "Excuse me for saying so but, in my opinion, your father did you a grave injustice. He taught you how to run a successful business, but he neglected to teach you that you have needs in your own right—that you have a duty to yourself and not just to his visions." Reaching out, he urged her chin toward him. "You are just as important as your responsibilities here at home and at the office. As you strive to meet everyone's needs, you mustn't forget yourself. You count, too, you know."

Zach walked toward them, and Geoffrey set his hands back on the arms of his chair. "All finished fishing?"

"We're giving up and going for ice cream."

Carrying the fishing rods and a pail, Sarah followed him. "We're just going to put this gear away and wash up. You'll come too, won't you?" Geoffrey turned and saw the usual protest in Meghan's brown eyes. "Come on. It sounds like fun."

"I'm driving, so you two will have the back seat."

Meghan raised her eyebrows at her sister. "You're taking that all-terrain thing that you use out on the beach? It doesn't even have a top."

Sarah's hazel eyes sparkled. "Yes, it's the perfect night for it. We'll be able to see the stars."

After ordering ice cream cones at the restaurant's walk-up window, Sarah and Zach wandered down to a little marshy area where crickets chirped and frogs croaked a medley of nocturnal sounds. Geoffrey led Meghan to a small picnic table, where he took a seat across from her. As he enjoyed his own cone, he watched in comfortable stillness as she licked vanilla ice cream from hers.

"You have a drop on your chin."

He handed her a napkin, and she wiped her mouth. "I can't remember the last time I had ice cream."

"One of the great treats of summer. You've been missing a lot."

He watched her bite into her cone. It crunched as she chewed. Then she hunched her shoulders and shivered.

"Cold?"

"A little."

Rising, he rounded the table and, straddling the bench, sat down beside her. When he slipped his arm around her and urged her toward him, she raised her eyes to meet his gaze.

Her light, warm breath, smelling of vanilla and sweetness, fanned across his cheek. He filled his lungs with moist night air and was acutely aware of her intoxicating nearness. Their faces were almost touching. He could see the tremor of her lips. Without considering the consequences of his action, he lowered his head and brushed his mouth against hers.

Sparks of sensation rushed through him and immobilized his rational mind. He thought he would explode from the intensity of feeling pulsing through him. Had Meghan felt it too?

"Ready to go, guys?" Geoffrey looked up to see Sarah giving them a curious stare. "It's getting a little chilly out here."

The following morning, Geoffrey rose after a sleepless night of tossing in bed thinking about Meghan. Every attempt he had made to clear his mind of her eyes, her thick, sweet smelling hair and full, tender lips had failed. He had spent the night remembering her feminine softness and the perfect way she fit into his arms.

Despite his best efforts, Meghan Blake had gotten to him, awakening a need in him that he had been managing to suppress for a long time. The quicker he removed himself from her presence, the better. He could not think when he was with her. Feelings of protectiveness and caring, that resembled his concept of love, plagued him with irritating regularity. Berating himself for having such lack of control over his emotions, he packed his bags and tidied the room he had used while staying at the Blake's house. Soon he would be on his way back to Boston and back to his own quiet life.

Yes, he had to return to his own world, to the life he knew, where Meghan Blake did not fill his dreams and complicate his days. He checked his watch and zipped his duffle bag. He had just time enough for coffee and toast before returning his car to the airport and catching his flight.

Setting his luggage in the foyer, he entered the dining room and smiled at Zach sitting at the table. His nephew looked up from the newspaper he was reading as Geoffrey took a seat across from him.

"All ready to head for the Cape?"

Helping himself to a cup of coffee from the pot on the table, he nodded. "Crashing waves and breathtaking sunsets and a deserted beach house are calling me."

He followed Zach's gaze. Sarah was hurrying into the dining room with a tense look on her face.

Zach rose from his seat. "Sarah, what is it? What's wrong?"

"Carly Hancock just called. She said that Meghan collapsed this morning at her office. A security guard found her and called for an ambulance to take her to the hospital."

Geoffrey jumped to his feet. "Collapsed? What happened?"

"I don't know. Carly didn't have any details. I need to go to her."

"Yes." Zach squeezed her hand. "I'll get the car."

"I'm coming with you." Geoffrey's mind raced as he followed the young couple out of the house.

For the second time in less than two weeks, he found himself alone and with a considerable lack of patience—not to mention his indescribable anxiety—in the waiting room of the hospital. As the minutes ticked by without a word from anyone, he grew restless. Frantic thoughts began to overwhelm his mind. If someone did not come soon to tell him how Meghan was doing, he would hunt down a doctor and demand some answers. *What is taking so long?*

He looked toward the doorway of the room as footsteps approached. "Zach, tell me what's going on. How is she?"

"I think she's going to be okay. She has a nasty cut, but it's not life threatening." He shook his head. "She's so stubborn, though. She keeps insisting there's nothing wrong."

"What happened?"

"She fell. The doctor says she's suffering from fatigue and stress. I guess he thinks there's something else wrong too, because he ordered some blood work."

"Blood work? For what?"

"I don't know. The results should be back in a few minutes."

"May I see her?"

He nodded. "Sarah asked me to get you. She thinks you might be able to help."

Geoffrey fell in step beside Zach as they hurried down the hospital corridor. "Help with what?"

"Talking some sense into the woman! Meghan's determined to leave. Apparently, she wants to catch a flight to New York City in a little while."

"What?"

"Yes, can you believe it? She just buried her grandmother. You'd think she could have at least taken the weekend off from work."

"I think she's going to have to postpone her trip."

"What about yours?" Zach made a left turn, and Geoffrey followed.

"I can't go now," he dragged his hand through his hair, "not until I'm sure Meghan's going to be all right."

His nephew grinned. "See, I told you. It's true love. It's got to be. You can't think of anything but being with her. I know the feeling exactly."

Geoffrey stopped and stared at Zach. At that moment, he realized that the younger man was absolutely right. He loved Meghan. He was *in* love with her. He thought about her day and night. Being with her scared him and excited him all at the same time. More than anything, he wanted to be with her, spend time with her, and learn everything he could about her.

When he and Zach entered a room filled with medical apparatus and supply cabinets, Geoffrey's eyes stared at the small, still woman sitting on the edge of the bed. His heart stopped.

Her face was ashen and her eyes, dull and listless. The gauze bandage covering her left cheek made him appreciate at once the gravity of the situation.

With effort, he forced himself to take steady breaths of air. If the feeling he was experiencing was love, then he was not sure he wanted anything to do with it. It was more painful than he ever imagined to see Meghan so pale and thin and vulnerable. He had been aware for days that she was not feeling well, but she looked drawn and exhausted. It seemed as though she had lost weight since the first time he had met her, less than a month ago, to discuss her interest in Wright Pharmaceuticals. Had her health deteriorated so much in such a short time? Should he have been more assertive and insisted that she seek medical attention?

"Meghan." He reached for her hands. "What happened?"

She shook her head. "It was dumb, Geoff. I fell and bumped my head. That's all." She glanced at Sarah and Zach standing at the foot of the bed. "I'm glad you're here. Finally, there's a voice of reason in this place. No one will listen. I'm just fine."

He studied the bruised skin around the edges of the bandage. "It looks like you had quite a tumble."

Sarah grasped his arm. "She did. Apparently, she fainted in her office and fell against one of Father's bronze sculptures. The security guard found her with a large gash on the left side of her face."

Meghan tried to slide from the bed, but Geoffrey stopped her. "Now, just wait a minute. You seem awfully shaky."

"She's supposed to be lying down with a cold cloth on her forehead."

"I don't have time for this, Sarah. I'm fine. I have to get to the airport." Her voice was so hoarse that they could barely hear her.

Geoffrey eased her shoulders back against a pillow and lifted her legs onto the bed. "Not right now, you don't. Just lie still." To his relief, a doctor strode into the examination room at that moment.

"Dr. Todd, this is Geoffrey Wright, my fiancè's uncle and a family friend. Is my sister going to be okay?"

Geoffrey shook the physician's hand as silent questions tumbled through his mind in agitated confusion. "I understand you've ordered some blood tests?"

The doctor nodded. "Miss Blake is dangerously dehydrated, and she is suffering from a slight concussion from the fall. The test results indicate she has enlarged lymph nodes and an abnormally high number of mononuclear leukocytes in her blood."

The words spun in Geoffrey's head, and a tight knot twisted in his stomach. Meghan rose into a sitting position. Sarah covered her mouth as an exclamation escaped.

"And what does that mean, Doctor?"

"Miss Blake has mononucleosis, Mr. Wright."

"I have what?"

Geoffrey slid an arm around Meghan's slim waist as she swayed toward the edge of the bed. "How serious is that?"

"It's very serious; but, with appropriate care, she should recover without complications. For the next few days, she'll need complete bed rest, careful monitoring of her symptoms and a proper diet."

Geoffrey glanced at Meghan, and her eyes pleaded with him. "I don't want to stay here, not where Grandma just died. I can't, Geoff."

Compassion washed over him, and he rubbed her uninjured cheek as he turned back to the doctor. "Do you have to admit her?"

"That won't be necessary as long as she avoids work for at least a week, gets plenty of bed rest and drinks enough liquids."

Sarah's tearful eyes widened. "Then she can go home?"

The physician nodded. "She needs to follow my instructions." He wagged a finger at Meghan. "Absolutely no stress. That means no work, no meetings and no trips to New York."

"What about medication?" Geoffrey said.

"I'll write out a prescription for a pain reliever and fever reducer. I can also give her a mild sedative, if she needs it.

Keep a close watch on her throat. If the swelling increases, I may have to administer cortisone." He patted Geoffrey's shoulder. "Unless complications arise, I won't have to see her again until a week from Monday. I'll decide then whether she will be able to return to work."

Sitting beside her in the back seat of the car on the ride from the hospital back to the Blake estate, Geoffrey watched Meghan's dark hair fall across the gauze bandage on her left cheek. With careful movements, he smoothed the silky, soft strands from her face and allowed himself to relax. His breathing had finally returned to normal. The sensation of an imaginary band tightening around his heart no longer tortured him. Meghan was going to be all right. She would recover from this miserable sickness that was trying to consume her—he would see to that.

Meghan awoke when they arrived at the house. After escorting her upstairs and into her bedroom, Geoffrey left her in Sarah's care while he went to the kitchen to see about lunch. Twenty minutes later, he balanced a tray of chicken soup, juice and tea as he ascended the curved staircase to the second floor of the mansion. Approaching Meghan's room on the south end of the corridor, he narrowly avoided spilling the contents of the tray down the front of him and onto the spotless hardwood floor as Sarah swept past him.

"What is it?" He searched her flushed face for assurance that Meghan was not in danger.

"It's hopeless." She threw her arms in the air. "She won't listen to a word I say."

Hurrying past the young woman, he stepped into the large bedroom with plain furnishings in muted brown and green tones. The wooden bed covered with a beige comforter was empty. He shook his head when he saw Meghan sitting at the nearby wooden desk. She held a telephone between her right shoulder and ear and supported a yellow legal pad of paper on her crossed legs as she wrote with a ball point pen.

Setting the tray on the desk, he placed his hand on her shoulder to obtain her attention. "The doctor said no work."

She covered the receiver with her palm. "He didn't say I couldn't talk. I need just a few more minutes with Carly."

"No more talk."

Her brown eyes widened in disbelief as he slid the telephone from her shoulder and lifted it to his mouth. "Carly, Miss Blake apologizes, but she needs to let you go now." As she stared at him, he replaced the receiver and removed the pen and pad from her hand.

"You can't do that!" Her indignation was almost lost in the pathetic rasping of her voice.

"What? See that you follow your doctor's orders?" He took her hand and helped her to her feet. "Apparently, you have no intention of doing so."

"I do. I just needed to take care of a few things."

"Well, now you're going to take care of you. It's time for lunch."

"Hey, great work, Geoff." In the doorway, Sarah clapped her hands. "You got that stupid phone away from her. Now, convince her to get into her pajamas. She ignores all of my suggestions."

Geoffrey lifted a blue cotton night shirt from the foot of the bed and leveled his eyes on Meghan's silent glare. "Go into the bathroom and change."

"I don't wear pajamas in the middle of the day."

"You do when you're sick. Now, go change. Your soup's getting cold."

When she hesitated, he felt a smile tug at the corner of his mouth. "I'll be happy to help you, my dear."

"I find no humor in this."

Her attempt to sustain her indignation failed—a hint of a smile brightened her pale face. "I can do it myself." She took the night shirt from his outstretched hand and crossed the floor to the adjacent bathroom.

"Hey, what just happened here?" With an expression of astonishment, Sarah stared at him. "You're amazing, Geoff. My sister doesn't let anyone tell her what to do. She's always in charge."

He chuckled. "I'm sure if she were feeling better, she wouldn't be letting me off so easily. Go have lunch with Zach. I'll see that Meghan eats and gets settled."

She chewed her bottom lip. "I'm really worried, Geoff. She never gets sick like this."

He gave the young woman a smile. "We'll help her do everything she needs to do to recover."

Sarah glanced with an anxious look at the closed bathroom door. "That's not going to be easy. She can be very stubborn."

He winked. "So can I."

Chapter Ten

"Geoff, come quick!"

He looked up from the book he was reading on the verandah when Sarah hurried through the door. Her face was flushed.

"Is Meghan awake?"

When she had emerged from the bathroom before lunch earlier that day, she was barefoot and wearing the blue night shirt that hung off her narrow shoulders and fell to her knees. She had slid into bed and had allowed him to prop up pillows behind her until she was comfortable enough to eat. After finishing her lunch in near silence, she had swallowed the tablets of prescription pain reliever that Geoffrey handed her and had leaned her head against the pillows and closed her eyes. He had waited for her to fall asleep and then left her alone.

"Oh, she's awake and more obstinate than you can imagine."

"I doubt that." He closed his book and rose to his feet. "She can't hurt herself too much in bed."

"But that's just the point. She's not in bed. She's not even in her bedroom."

"Where is she?"

"I caught her in her study faxing reports to Carly. Right now, she's composing an agenda for a meeting she's set up for Monday morning in Richmond."

"What?" Shaking his head, he rushed to the study without waiting for a response.

He took long strides fueled by annoyance toward the study. Meghan sat at her desk in front of the French doors overlooking the yard as she typed.

He flattened his hands on her blotter, which was covered with piles of manila folders and reports. "Do you want to kill yourself? Is that your objective?"

She kept her eyes focused on the monitor. "I feel much better."

"Your doctor says you need to rest."

"I have some work to do. I promise I'll go back to bed as soon as I'm finished."

Straightening, he stuffed his clenched fists into the pockets of his pants as he tried to control his temper. "You agreed to the doctor's conditions."

"Only because I couldn't face the idea of staying in the hospital."

"You'll be right back there if you're not careful. I'll take you there myself."

She leaned around the side of the monitor and smiled at him. "Is that a threat, Mr. Wright?"

His anger dissipated as he looked at her, and he softened his scowl. "Not a threat, exactly. I just want you to get better, Meghan."

"I am. I told you. Don't I look better?"

He rounded the desk and turned her wheeled leather chair toward him. She looked so pale and exhausted that his heart tightened in his chest, and his frustration melted into compassion and tenderness. She wore a plain cotton robe to cover her over-sized nightshirt, and her feet were encased in white cotton socks. The model figure of a successful business executive, she was not. Squatting beside her chair, he gazed into her brown eyes. Seeing her so ill and vulnerable caused an inexplicable pull in the pit of his stomach. He inhaled a ragged breath.

"Meghan, be reasonable. We're all trying to help you get better."

"I'm fine." She clicked the mouse and set the printer next to the computer into motion.

He reached out and took her chin between his gentle fingers. "You're not fine. You're sick, and denying that fact is not going to improve your health. You're worrying all of us, especially Sarah."

"I can't be sick, Geoff." Her voice was a whisper.

He knew he had not imagined the trembling of her chin. Was it possible that the powerful president of Blake Industries was scared?

"My father put me in charge. He counted on me to take care of things." Her brown eyes were huge and glassy as she looked at him. "Getting sick would let him down."

He rubbed his fingers against her right cheek as he chose his words with care. He had a difficult time accepting that this powerful adult woman was so affected by her dead parent.

"There are plenty of employees on your staff at Blake Industries to handle the day-to-day affairs. Knowing your meticulous nature, you would have trained them well. I think you need to relax and let them do the jobs you hired them to do. You deserve this time to let yourself get better." He watched her close her eyes as she heaved a sigh. He used the opportunity to turn off the computer. "I want you to go back upstairs and get into bed. You need to rest." He massaged her slender shoulders. "What would you like for dinner?"

"I'm not hungry."

"You have to eat, Meghan. How about some hot cereal?"

She swallowed, and he saw her wince. "Why do you bother with me, Geoff? Why are you so nice?"

"Because I care." With a gentle tug, he pulled her to her feet. "You go get settled in bed, and I'll have Sarah bring dinner right up to you." He watched with relief as she did not protest, and padded across the study in her white socks.

Hours later, the image of Meghan in her robe crossing the study floor with obvious reluctance remained etched into Geoffrey's mind. He punched his pillow at the head of his bed and rolled onto his back. He stared into the darkness as a clear picture of her large dark eyes stared back at him. Exhaling a ragged breath, he willed the minutes of the night to pass with merciful quickness while the enchanting powers of Meghan Blake seemed to take possession of his heart and squeeze until he could no longer breathe or think rational thoughts.

A rapid pounding on the door of his room caused him to bolt up in the bed. "Yes, yes, what is it?" He grabbed his robe and hurried across the room.

He knew from Sarah's pale face and scared green eyes that something was wrong. "Meghan collapsed again. She's in the foyer."

Without giving him a chance to respond, she turned and ran down the corridor to the staircase. Geoffrey followed her.

Meghan was sitting in a large chair in the bright hallway when they reached the bottom step. Zach was leaning over her as she held her head between her knees

"Why is she out of bed? Did she fall?" Geoffrey searched first Zach's and then Sarah's face as concern gripped his chest. The whole scene confused him. It was 2:00 in the morning, and Meghan should have been asleep in her pajamas in bed—but she was not. She was downstairs, trembling in a chair with her head between her legs, and wearing a navy dress with buttons all the way down the front of it. What was going on?

"I couldn't sleep," Sarah rubbed Meghan's back. "I came down to get a glass of milk, and I heard a car in the driveway. Apparently, Meghan was on her way to the office and left her car running while she came back into the house for something. I caught her walking through the front door."

Meghan lifted her head, and Geoffrey was shocked by the sight of her sunken eyes and white face. When she spoke, her voice was a ragged whisper. "I forgot my meeting agenda for Monday."

"Are you crazy?" He did not try to curb the anger in his voice. "You also forgot that you're in no shape to drive. And why in the world were you going to your office in the middle of the night?"

"She fainted, Geoff," Zach said. "I heard Sarah scream, and I ran downstairs. Meghan fell again, but I don't think she's hurt."

Geoffrey swallowed his anger and kneeled in front of her. "How do you feel now? Are you well enough to go back upstairs?"

She raised her head. "The car—"

"Forget the car, Meghan. It's you we're concerned about."

"I'll put it away," Zach said. He tossed Geoffrey a look of concern before he headed toward the front door.

"Can you stand, Meghan?"

Geoffrey watched as she tried to rise on unsteady legs. He caught her arm when she fell back into the chair. With one smooth motion, he lifted her into his arms and headed toward the stairs. With very little physical effort, Geoffrey reached the top of the stairs and carried her down the hallway to her bedroom. As he set her on the edge of the bed, he rehearsed his words. He wanted to make sure he controlled the fear and anger he was experiencing.

Sitting next to her, he took her hand in his. "You heard the doctor, Meghan. The mononucleosis you have is making you very sick." He inhaled a deep breath. "You need to rest. If you want to continue to run Blake Industries, then you're going to have to take some time off right now and let your body heal. You don't have a choice, Meghan."

Gazing into her glassy brown eyes, he said, "I won't let you die."

"I'm not going to die, Geoff."

"You're not going to improve if you don't start making better decisions. What were you thinking when you decided to drive to Newport News in the middle of the night?"

She shrugged a trembling shoulder. "I do it all the time."

"What? Go to your office at 2:00 in the morning? Meghan, that's insane. It's a wonder you haven't gotten sick before now." He met her eyes with a piercing gaze. "You do realize, don't you, that you will have to discontinue this intensely demanding work schedule of yours. It's impossible to keep such a grueling pace without your health eventually suffering."

"My father did it."

"And he died of a heart attack at forty-eight. You need to start taking care of yourself, Meghan, and the first step right now is to get back to bed."

He picked up her nightshirt that was hanging over the side of the bed. "Put this back on."

Nodding, she attempted to rise but swayed and grabbed his arm. "I don't think I can. I feel so weak."

"Okay, just take it easy." Guiding her down on the edge of the bed, he said a silent prayer of thanks that Sarah had found Meghan before she had had a chance to drive away in her car. He did not know what he would have done if she had fainted and driven into a ditch, or if something even worse had happened to her in her condition.

He pulled the nightshirt over her head and watched her fumble with the row of buttons on the front of her dress. "Here, let me do that." With his own fingers trembling, he unfastened the navy garment and slipped it off.

He adjusted the nightshirt over her thin shoulders, and she slid her arms into the sleeves. He watched the worn fabric fall to her knees. "Lie back, and I'll cover you up."

He pulled the comforter up to her chin and tucked it around her. His chest tightened as he looked at the fragile, vulnerable woman who had come to mean so much to him. With a sigh, he reached out and brushed back strands of brown hair from her pale face. He waited for her to close her eyes. When her steady, rhythmic breathing told him she was asleep, he tiptoed from the room. Closing the door, he was surprised to meet Sarah and Zach standing outside of Meghan's room.

"How is she? She's okay, isn't she?" Sarah's green eyes stared at him as she caught his arm.

"She's asleep now, but we can't be sure for how long. Your sister is determined to do what she wants, in spite of how it will affect her health."

"What can we do?" Zach asked, slipping his arm around Sarah's waist. "At this rate, Meghan's never going to get better."

"She needs a place where there's no work and no telephone and no computer," Sarah added.

"But, sweetheart, where is such a place? The beach house is peaceful and isolated, but it's full of telephones, and Meghan has a computer there."

The young woman's hazel eyes grew thoughtful. "You know, that just might work. You're a genius, Zach."

She turned to Geoffrey and squeezed his arm. "Will you help, Geoff? We have to do something. Meghan can't go on like this—sneaking off to work and using the computer and talking on the telephone. It's too hard for us to watch her here."

"I agree with you, Sarah, but I don't know what I can possibly do. I've been miserably ineffective so far."

"No, you haven't. At least she listens to you. Will you take Meghan to the beach house for the week? I need your help. Meghan's always been the strong one who took care of me. Now, she needs me, and she won't let me help her. Will you help, please?"

Zach drew her close to him. "What's your plan? What about the telephones?"

"We can disconnect the telephone and internet lines down there and find a safe place for her cell phone and pager. Geoff can take Meghan down by himself. You and I can stay here and finish up the work recording the memorial donations and writing out all of the thank you notes for the flowers and gifts. We'll keep in touch with Geoff on his own cell phone. A week should be enough time to see some improvement in her condition. If she's better by the weekend, we'll go down then. What do you think, Geoff?"

"Oh, I don't know, Sarah—"

"I'll do anything you say and give you anything you need. Just do what you have to do to get her well again."

Zach shook his head. "That'll put Geoff in an awkward position. Keeping Meghan from work and telephones and computers is going to make her very unhappy."

Sarah shrugged. "It's either Hatteras Island or the hospital. I think she would choose the beach house. Anyway, Geoff can handle her. I've seen him do it."

Geoffrey sighed. "I'm glad to have your confidence, Sarah. Do you think this is the only way to help her?"

"I think it is. Now what can I do to make things easier for you?"

Thoughts raced through his mind. "First, you'll have to contact Carly Hancock and explain that Meghan will be on vacation for at least a week. Your sister is highly sensitive about her health, so I don't think she would want everyone in the office knowing that she's ill. Have Carly reschedule all meetings and business trips until further notice. Tell her to hold all calls, papers and reports for Meghan until she returns to work. I'm sure that a major company like Blake Industries can run smoothly for five days without its president's constant physical presence at the office."

"What if there is an emergency?"

He inhaled a deep breath. "We'll just have to face that problem if and when it happens, Sarah; but, for Meghan's sake, I hope it doesn't. Right now she needs to focus all of her energy and attention on getting better."

"What can I do?" Zach said.

"Pack my rental car with food and supplies for at least a week. I don't want to have to leave Meghan alone or to drag her shopping with me. I'll drive down to Waves with her tomorrow morning."

Sarah threw her arms around Geoffrey's neck. "Oh, thank you so much. I appreciate you helping us through this. Someday Meghan will thank you too."

"Don't count on that. She'll probably never forgive me for this."

"Of course she will. We'll both be forever in your debt."

"Geoff doesn't need payment, Sarah. He's doing this out of love."

"Love? What are you talking about?" Her head swung from Zach to Geoffrey. "You're in love with Meghan? Really? She's never even had a steady boyfriend that I'm aware of."

Zach grinned. "Well, I guess she does now."

"Wow, this is just amazing." Sarah took a few steps from them.

Geoffrey cleared his throat. "This is a discussion that can wait for another time. If we're set until tomorrow morning, I think we should all try to get some sleep."

"Will Meghan stay in her room, or do you think we should take shifts standing guard?"

"Geoff will be on constant vigilance for a week if he's going to be at the beach house alone with Meghan," Zach said. "I'll stay awake and keep an eye on her until morning. You two go ahead and get some rest."

"Are you sure? I don't mind."

Zach kissed Sarah's cheek. "Yes, I'll sleep tomorrow after Geoff heads out to Hatteras."

"You're both being so nice." Sarah's chin trembled. "I don't know how I would have gotten through all of this without you. Except for you, Meghan is all the family I have left."

Geoffrey reached out and squeezed her arm. "Hey, take it easy, Sarah. Things are going to be okay. Meghan will get better. We'll all get through this ordeal together because we are your family now. Go to bed."

Despite Geoffrey's grave concern that Meghan would protest any move to the beach house on Sunday morning, she awoke with such a sore throat and headache that she did little more than nod and shake her head occasionally as they all helped her pack the personal items she would need for the next few days. With a sense of hope that a plan was now in place to help Meghan recover from the terrible sickness that was weakening both her mind and body, Geoffrey made the drive with more optimism than he had had in days.

Although Meghan slept most of the ride with her head resting on a pillow against the back of the car seat, he pulled off the road several times to check on her and to make sure she drank small sips of water at regular intervals. When they arrived in Waves, the morning sun was hot in a cloudless sky—a perfect day to be at the beach—but he led her inside and took her at once to her bedroom. Playing in the sand and the ocean would just have to wait until she recovered.

For three days, the time passed without any significant event. To Geoffrey's relief, Meghan slept most of the time. During the few hours each day when she was awake, she drank small amounts of liquids and ate even smaller amounts of food. She took long baths twice a day and changed into clean pajamas before going back to sleep.

He called Sarah on Tuesday evening after Meghan had fallen asleep. So far, she had not tried to sneak into the den to do work or to find a telephone or keys to his car.

"How is she? Do you see any improvements?"

"I think you'd be surprised. She getting both color and strength back."

"What about her throat? Has the swelling gone down?"

"Not noticeably, but the doctor said it would take a few days. She eating and drinking regularly. Today she had some scrambled eggs and a cup of soup."

"That doesn't sound like much."

"It's more than she was eating. Give her time, Sarah. How are you and Zach doing?"

"Great. Zach had a job interview today at Blake Industries. Of course, he was told that the final decision would be Meghan's when she returns from her vacation; but Joseph Cohen, one of the vice presidents, really liked his resume and portfolio. We're so excited."

"Tell Zach I'll be thinking about him. Any problems at the office?"

"None. As you know, I call Carly every few hours or stop by her office to see what's going on. Things have been quiet, thank goodness. Carly told everyone that Meghan wanted to take some time off after Grandma's death and has been careful not to go into details about her health."

"That's good. Meghan would be furious if she thought we shared her private affairs at work."

"My sister is finally getting a lesson in the natural weaknesses all we humans have. Finally, she'll have to realize that she's one of us and not some kind of super woman."

"That might not happen right away, Sarah." He chuckled. "Meghan hasn't talked much, but she's asked about you."

"Really? Maybe she even misses me! If you don't think it'll be too much for her, we'll drive out Friday afternoon. I'd like to keep it kind of quiet for this weekend, though, so Zach and I don't plan to invite anyone else."

"That's a good idea. I think you'll be pleased when you see how well she's coming along."

"Just watch out, Geoff. As soon as she starts to feel better, she'll be right back to her old tricks. And she'll probably be absolutely miserable to you until you let her have her way."

"Are you losing confidence in your belief that I can handle your sister?"

"No, just the opposite. I think you're the only one who can, Geoff. I just want you to be careful. Good luck, and I'll talk with you tomorrow."

At lunch the following day, Meghan emerged from her bedroom dressed and more alert than Geoffrey had seen her in days. As she approached him in the hallway, he noted that the hair brushing her shoulders was damp from her shower, and her skin was glowing with a healthy pink hue that contrasted sharply with the memory he had of her in his arms the night he carried her upstairs and set her on her bed after she had tried to drive to her office in Newport News.

"Well, good afternoon, my dear." He was unable to curb the feeling of pure elation that welled up inside of him at the sight of her. "Are you hungry?"

When she nodded, a slight smile lit up her face. Her outfit was bright and crisp and reminded him of a summer day on Cape Cod. In lime green capri pants and yellow sleeveless sweater, she appeared ready for the beach.

"Come with me." He beckoned with his hand. "Let's go make some lunch."

As he pulled a bowl, measuring cups and spoons, and mixing utensils from various cupboards in the spacious kitchen, Meghan slid onto the high stool at the bar that separated the food preparation area from an informal dining room lined with sliding glass doors that led to a balcony overlooking the pool. He measured flour, butter, sugar and milk into the bowl and then searched a nearby cupboard for additional ingredients.

"What may I do?"

Surprised, he pushed the bowl toward her and held out a large wooden spoon. "You mix, but not too much."

"What are we making?"

"Cranberry muffins, if I can find the cranberries I asked Zach to pack."

"Cranberries in North Carolina? You travel with your native food?"

Geoffrey grinned at her. "I was born and raised in eastern Massachusetts. You must know that cranberries are practically a staple there. Don't you like cranberries?"

"Yes, I do." She nodded. "But you're in the South now. You should be preparing specialties of this area of the country."

"Like what? I'm not sure seafood would taste very good in muffins."

She wrinkled her nose, and his heart skipped a beat.

"Clam cakes are delicious, but that's not what I had in mind. There used to be blueberry bushes down by the cove at home."

"Blueberry muffins. Now, they sound good. You'll have to show me when we get back."

She looked into the bowl as if concentrating her whole attention on the lumpy mixture. "I'm not even sure the bushes are still there. It's been years since I've picked them."

As she stirred, he threw a handful of dried cranberries into the bowl and then set a muffin tin on the counter. "If you'll get those ready for the oven, I'll work on the chicken salad."

An hour later, Meghan licked muffin crumbs from her fingertips and then wiped her hands with a napkin. "I never realized that food could taste so good. What's for dessert?"

"Dessert?" Geoffrey raised an eyebrow at her. "You must be feeling better. If you keep eating like this, you'll have to buy bigger clothes."

"That's not even close to funny." Her large brown eyes sparkled with amusement. "Is there dessert or not?"

"There is." He slid off the bar stool and set their plates on the counter next to the dishwasher. "I made a treat my mother always made for me when I wasn't feeling well."

Pulling two clear parfait glasses from the refrigerator, he carried them to the bar and set one in front of Meghan. "Tapioca pudding layered with whipped cream and topped with caramel sauce."

"Ooh." She dipped a long handled spoon into the glass. "What a spoiled child you must have been." She swallowed a generous spoonful. "You probably pretended to be sick just to get some of your mother's treats like this."

"Never." He winked at her. "I didn't lie. I was a perfect child."

"Who grew up to be a perfect man?"

"I didn't say that."

She inhaled a deep breath as she licked first the front and then the back of the spoon. "I should thank you for being so nice to me."

"It's been my pleasure, Meghan."

"I feel a bit spoiled myself."

"Such a hard-working woman deserves a little pampering once in awhile."

She tipped her head to one side as she held her spoon in the air. "I should be taking care of myself."

He smiled. "There's certainly nothing wrong with that, but everyone needs someone to lean on occasionally. You must face extraordinary challenges every day, but you often doubt your own worth. I believe you need, and deserve, the kind of unconditional love from others that will help you to acknowledge your own personal merits above and beyond your success in the business world."

He watched her brown eyes appear to fill with doubt as she listened to his words. "Love without conditions. I'm not sure that's real."

Reaching across the bar, he brushed his fingertips along her left cheek, where the bruise and cut were nearly healed. "It most definitely is, my dear, and someday I hope you'll grow to realize that. Now, you look as though you're going to fall asleep right here. Go rest, and I'll clean up the kitchen."

"I can help first." After covering a yawn with her hand, she gave him a sheepish grin. "I guess I am a bit tired."

After he loaded the dishwasher, wiped the counters and put away the leftover food, Geoffrey wandered to the third floor to check on Meghan in her bedroom. The beach house was quiet—so different from the holiday weekend when Hilary Blake and her nurse and all of Sarah and Zach's lively friends had been there, filling the rooms with activity and laughter.

When he glanced through Meghan's open doorway and found her room empty, concern washed over him. Sarah's words from the previous evening rushed through his mind. Taking two steps at a time, he hurried down to the den, but he found it empty too. As he stared at the vacant desk chair, his panic increased. The car! Had she found his keys and taken it while he was in the kitchen?

When he checked the parking area below the house and found his car right where he had left it Sunday morning, he breathed a momentary sigh of relief. Worries replaced it, though, as he returned to the main floor of the beach house and strode with determination to the living room. He hoped that she had not gone to the beach alone, without a hat or sunscreen. Her pale skin would certainly be burned in minutes in the afternoon sun rays. She was still unsteady on her feet, and walking alone in the sand would be difficult for her.

His eyes scanned the comfortable room as he willed his thoughts to remain calm and clear. When he finally saw her curled up in a corner of one of the sofas, his heart stopped. He thought his legs would collapse from the rush of relief flooding through his body.

A strand of hair fell over her cheek as her head rested on a beige pillow. With her knees bent and her arms folded around her, she appeared relaxed and comfortable and without a single thought of work. With emotion that he could not identify welling up inside of him, Geoffrey watched her for several moments as she slept. He crossed the room on unsteady legs and pulled a light cotton blanket from the back of a nearby chair. With slow, careful movements, he draped the blanket over her and held his breath, waiting to see if covering her up had disturbed her.

While her breathing continued its steady rhythm, he

stepped away from the sofa toward the bookshelves lining one wall of the room. After selecting a suspense novel, he settled in a cozy chair where he could look out of the sliding glass doors at the sand dunes and beach and clear blue summer sky.

When Meghan stirred hours later, she opened her eyes and gazed at him. Her head remained on the pillow as she stretched her legs out to their full length on the sofa. "You look wonderfully comfortable over there."

He looked up from the book on his lap and smiled at her. "So do you."

"I can't understand why I'm sleeping so much." She stretched her arms above her head. "Are you reading anything exciting?"

He nodded. "Cold War espionage. It's excellent."

"What a luxury. I can't remember the last time I read a book for simple pleasure."

"Leisure reading isn't a luxury for me. It's a necessity." He waved his hand toward the wall of books. "Why don't you pick something out? You have time to read now."

She shrugged her slender shoulders and swung her legs onto the floor. "Good idea. I think I will."

She read for awhile and then dozed and then read again. From his chair, Geoffrey noticed that although she seemed to want to be more active, her body continued to require rest. Her usual level of energy was still waning. She had not completely recovered yet.

Sometime later, he watched her close her book and cross the floor to gaze out at the surf and sky. He set his own book on a nearby stand and looked at her back. He fought his desire to go to her and to draw her into his arms. His mind refused to forget how she had felt as they danced together at the restaurant. He wanted to dance with her again.

"Shall I prepare dinner?" He forced himself to remain seated as the physical need to touch her threatened to over-whelm his rational thought.

"Why?" She tossed him a teasing glance. "So you can make fun of my appetite again?"

"I promise I won't say a thing."

She shook her head. "I'm really not hungry." He watched her wander around to one side of the room, where wooden doors with brass knobs lined the walls. She opened one door and perused the contents of the storage cabinet before clos-ing it and moving on the the next door.

"Are you looking for something?"

"Grandma used to store her paints and supplies in one of these closets. She opened a third door. "Here they are."

Swinging the door open, Meghan lowered herself onto the floor in front of the neatly stocked shelves and, sitting with her legs crossed, began to pull tubes of paint, brushes, sketch pads and canvases from the cabinet. She worked in silence for several minutes as she searched through boxes, and wooden and plastic containers of art supplies.

"Grandma loved art." She picked through a tin case of colored pencils. "It was one of her special passions."

He leaned toward her until he could look over her shoul-ders. "Have you been thinking a lot about your grandmother?"

She snapped the pencil box shut and nodded as strands of brunette hair fell forward and partially hid her face. "She's been in my dreams, strong and vibrant and responsive, just the way I remember her years ago. She seems very real sometimes. I wake up believing she is still alive, but then I feel like my heart will break when I realize she's not there. I miss her so much."

Although he could not see her face, he thought her shoul-ders were shaking as though she were crying. He knew for sure when tear drops began to dampen the lid of the pencil box in her lap. He reached out and rubbed her upper arms with his hands.

"Before she died, it had been months since Grandma even recognized me. I thought I had done all of my grieving for her then."

Her quiet voice caught in her throat, and he felt her shiver. Setting aside his book, he sat down on the floor behind her and wrapped his arms around her trembling body. Her initial stiffness melted into silent acceptance of his offered comfort. She nestled against his chest as tears flowed from her eyes, from the very depths of her soul. While she clung to him, her sobs became whimpers, and her whimpers became quiet sighs until her breathing relaxed into a steady rhythm once again.

He did not say a word. He simply held her until the pain of her grief subsided, hoping that he was providing even the slightest emotional support in such a time of personal sorrow and distress.

Chapter Eleven

Geoffrey did not see Meghan awake again until Thursday morning, when she rushed into the kitchen while he was pouring a cup of coffee. After returning the pot to its warming burner, he looked up at her standing in the doorway.

Surprised to see her dressed in a dark blue skirt and matching jacket, he frowned. She must have kept the suit at the beach house because he knew that Sarah had not packed any sort of business clothes for her sister.

"Good morning. Did you sleep well?"

"Geoffrey, I need to make some telephone calls."

"No, you don't."

Still glassy, her eyes had begun to recapture some of their usual sheen. "Will you please explain to me why every phone in this house is disconnected?"

"Sarah did it so you could rest and wouldn't be enticed to contact your office."

A shadow of confusion crossed her pale face. "What day is today?"

"Thursday."

She caught her lower lip between her teeth. "I thought it was Monday. It's really Thursday?"

When she slumped against the doorway, he rushed to her side. "We came down Sunday. You've been very sick, Meghan. Don't you remember?"

She pressed her fingers to her temples. "How could I have lost so many days?"

He slipped his arm around her waist. "You needed sleep and just weren't aware that time was passing. Come, sit down." He led her to a stool by the bar. "It's understandable that you're confused. Would you like some juice?"

She shook her head. "I haven't been to the office all week?"

"You needed some time off from work."

She covered her eyes with her hands. "What can the office possibly be thinking about my unexplained absence?"

"That you're taking some time off."

She narrowed her eyes at him. "I need a phone to call Carly."

"No."

"No?"

"No, you may not use my phone."

"Geoff, I'm not playing games. I have to call my office."

"Your office is doing fine. Sarah and Carly have spoken every day. Your staff is not expecting you back until you see the doctor next Monday. You're not supposed to work until then, remember?"

Her brown eyes grew large and round. "But I feel better."

He set his hands on her shoulders. "Listen, Meghan. I know this is difficult for you."

"Difficult! Geoffrey Wright, I have a business to run. I need a phone."

He shook his head, remembering Sarah's warning that he must be firm with her sister. "No phone."

"I promise to make only one call. Please."

Geoffrey met her pleading eyes. "You're not going to make any calls, Meghan."

Her jaw tightened. "Give me the phone."

"No."

Squaring her shoulders, she glared at him. "If you deny me access to a telephone, then I'll use your car keys to drive to one."

"You're not driving anywhere either, Meghan."

She set her hands on her hips. "Are you holding me prisoner here?"

"Of course not. I'll take your anywhere you want to go."

"Anywhere?"

She'll be absolutely miserable to you until you let her have her way. Sarah's words filled his mind as his determination waned. This situation was not going to be an easy one.

"Anywhere within reason, Meghan. I'm not taking you to your office in Newport News or to the airport to fly to New York or to any place where you will be able to sneak a phone call to your secretary or executive assistant."

She glared at him. "I despise you, Geoffrey Wright. You're being completely unfair."

"Maybe, but you're getting better, and that's what counts. Regardless of your opinion of my methods, you can't deny that you're making progress toward recovery. I don't think that would be happening if you were still following that incredible schedule of yours."

Her brown eyes brightened for a moment. "One call won't hurt."

He rubbed her cheek with the back of his hand. "I see that you have two choices, my dear. You can mope around here complaining about how you're being mistreated and not getting your own way, or you can come and enjoy this beautiful day on Hatteras Island with me."

Forcing himself to avoid her eyes, he reached for his coffee mug, turned, and left the room. He knew that if he stayed, those big brown eyes and her persuasive pleading would wear him down until she got her way. He had to be firm, for her own health and well-being. If he could hold out for just a few more days and stick with the plan he and Sarah had devised to help Meghan, then soon she would be strong enough to return to her demanding work schedule and what she considered a "normal" life.

As he strode, with determined steps, toward one of the upstairs balconies, he realized that his life, on the other hand, would never be normal again. No matter how many times he told himself how hopeless it was, he knew, without a doubt, that he was in love with Meghan; but she despised him. That is what she had said, and her words hurt more than any real physical pain he had ever experienced.

He refused to deceive himself with false hopes of a future that included Meghan as more than his nephew's sister-in-law. She was not interested in him. She did not even like him. There was really no sense in dreaming about spending the rest of his life with her. With a heavy heart, he finished his coffee and headed to his room to change. He knew that the only remedy for his troubled mind would be a strenuous swim in the pool. He would not let Meghan's refusal of his invitation to enjoy the day curtail his own attempts to bask in the beautiful summer sun of the Outer Banks.

He was just about to pull himself from the refreshing depths of the Blake beach house pool when Meghan appeared again—this time in a light pink cotton dress and sandals. She descended the stairs from the floor above the swim area. As she crossed the tiled deck, he watched the skirt of her long dress brush her ankles and then allowed his eyes to roam upward to her face. She had pulled her hair back into a pink fabric elastic band at her nape. Her brown eyes were large and round on her pale face.

Taking a moment to steady his heart beat, he rested his elbows on the edge of the pool and then gave her a cautious smile. He could not tell by the carefully veiled expression on her face if she was still angry about their earlier conversation. "I don't suppose you'd like to join me for a swim?"

She shook her head. "Is swimming the only activity you had planned for today?"

"No." He pulled himself into a sitting position onto the edge of the pool. "I thought we could take a drive down to the south end of the island and browse through some of the shops in Hatteras village that Sarah told me about, and we could have lunch on the beach there. Do you think you're up for such an excursion?"

Her smiled warmed his taut nerves. Had she forgiven him?

"That sounds like fun." She took a seat on the edge of a lounge chair. "But since I've been sleeping so much these past few days, I can't guarantee I won't need a nap or two at some point during the trip."

He could not hide his elation. "Give me ten minutes to shower and dress, and I'll be ready." Grabbing his towel from the back of another lounge chair, he hurried into the house.

After the initial shock of learning that she had been alone with Geoffrey on Hatteras Island for over four days—during which she had barely been conscious—Meghan began to allow herself to relax, and to enjoy the peace and warmth that seemed to envelope her whenever she was with him. She did, after all, feel better; and because no one else was staying at the beach house, she assumed that he had been the one instrumental in nursing her back to health.

Although she had been furious with him for refusing to give her access to a telephone, she discovered that she could not stay angry at him for very long. If fact, as they strolled in and out of little specialty boutiques and souvenir shops, she became increasingly aware of her acceptance of his quiet presence. Without understanding why, she grew to anticipate with pleasure the gentle touch of his hand on her elbow as he guided her around other shoppers, or his intense gray eyes catching her gaze over store displays to share some unique treasure he found amusing or interesting.

When Geoffrey suggested they leave the stores and cross a nearby boardwalk to the beach, she welcomed his offer with enthusiasm. The idea of sharing the fresh sea air and picnic lunch with him caused her heart to race. Why?

After placing a large umbrella in the sand, to shade them from the most direct afternoon sun, and making sure she had a comfortable seat on the blanket he had spread out near the base of some dunes covered with waving sea oats, he pulled several plastic containers from a thermal picnic bag and set a feast before her. As she watched him, she realized that he would not have had time to pack such a bag after his swim in the pool. Had he been so sure she would accept his invitation to spend the day with him? It amazed her that, at times, he seemed to know her better than she knew herself.

Removing her sunglasses and setting them on the blanket next to her, she took a bite of cheese and cracker and watched the way the wind played with strands of his dark hair. Her heart skipped a beat as he combed them back with his hand before popping a plump purple grape into his mouth. Smiling, he held out the bowl of fruit to her.

Had she noticed before the strong line of his jaw or the way his eyes seemed to sparkle with delight when she smiled, or thanked him for some kind gesture? His compassion and intelligence had always amazed her; but today, his classic handsome features took away her breath whenever she looked at him. He always appeared so unpretentious and at ease with himself and his life. With reluctance, she dragged her eyes from her intriguing companion and turned her concentration back to lunch.

She selected bottled spring water over the sparkling mineral water Geoffrey offered because she was afraid the carbonation would irritate her healing, yet still extremely sore, throat. She ate more cheese and crackers and munched sweet, sun-warmed fruit. The food tasted so good to her.

"Delicious." She wiped her hands on a paper napkin and leaned back against the pillows Geoffrey had piled behind her.

"Dessert?" He held out another plastic container. "Shortbread cookies. I hope you like these. They're my favorite."

Choosing a light square cookie, she met his eyes as she nibbled the crumbly treat. "Grandma used to buy these for me when I was a little girl. They're yummy."

His soft chuckle elicited a series of butterfly flutters in her stomach. "What's so funny?"

He shook his dark head. "Sometimes, Meghan, you are pure delight."

"That sounds like the name of a mouthwatering dessert."

His gray eyes sparkled. "I think the president of Blake Industries should take a few more days off to go window shopping and to eat shortbread cookies. You don't use words like 'yummy' nearly as often as you should."

His grin sent a flood of warmth through her, and she laughed. "I can just picture it. Good afternoon, members of the board. Help yourselves to some yummy pastries and bagels before we begin our meeting. The coffee is decaf, so we'll all sleep well tonight."

His grin widened. "That sounds perfectly executive-like to me." With his index finger, he reached out and touched the corner of her mouth. "You have a crumb."

His fingertip lingered on her skin, sending ripples of electricity through her. Disappointment followed as he pulled away his hand. Meghan inhaled quick shallow breaths as the simple action created an unsolicited thought, not only of fingertips, but of his lips on that same corner of her mouth—the corner that still tingled from his touch. She could not understand why her skin refused to forget it even moments after he had removed his finger.

"What?" She brushed her hand across her mouth as he continued to look at her. "More crumbs?"

"No, I'm admiring."

"Admiring what?"

"You, Meghan. You're lovely."

She rolled her eyes. "Oh, yes. Ashen skin tone and big dark circles under one's eyes are in fashion this season."

"You're starting to get some color back."

When he leaned toward her, her heart quickened. She breathed in his fresh, clean cologne and unique masculine scent as faint but undeniable sparks of excitement ignited in the pit of her stomach and caught her by surprise. When his tender lips brushed against hers, her mind filled with thoughts of fairy tales and happy endings. All too soon, he pulled away and held out his hand to her.

"Come with me. Let's go for a walk. I need some exercise."

Inhaling a long, calming breath, she allowed him to help her to her feet. She closed her eyes for a moment in an attempt to steady her legs as well as her nerves.

"Do you feel faint?" The concern was obvious in his voice.

She shook her head and gazed at the huge powerful ocean to avoid his searching gray eyes. "No, I'm okay now."

Lacing his fingers with hers, he kicked off his deck shoes

and urged her down toward the water. The sea air filled her with energy and serenity. She could not imagine a more perfect day. The sound of the surf, the fragrance of the sea and the awesome expanse of the nearly deserted beach filled her with a sense of wonder and satisfaction that she had not experienced since her childhood. After days of confinement and complete lack of awareness of the world around her, her senses craved stimulation.

Geoffrey's gentleness and consideration all afternoon held a mysterious appeal for her. Despite her attempt to ignore it, she was beginning to crave his presence and attention. Never before had she wished time would stand still so she could enjoy a day or an afternoon or even an hour away from her work, but today she found herself enjoying both the wonders of nature and the pleasant rapport of a man who no longer seemed like a stranger, but a caring and supporting friend.

Later that afternoon, Geoffrey held open the door of the beach house as Meghan covered a yawn with her hand and entered the hallway leading to the main floor. "I managed to stay awake all afternoon, but now I feel very sleepy. I'm sorry."

"Don't apologize." He set the picnic bag, pillows and blankets on a nearby counter. "We probably did too much today. I'm afraid I was having too much fun to stop." He gave her one of his irresistible smiles. "I had a wonderful time, Meghan."

Warm feelings of contentment flowed through her. "Me, too. You have an incredible ability to distract me from all thoughts of work, something I never imagined was possible. I'm not sure I've ever felt so relaxed."

She held her breath as he leaned toward her and kissed her cheek. "Go, enjoy your nap."

When she awoke again hours later and went in search of him, she found Geoffrey on his way to the pool for an early evening swim. The sight of his bare, bronzed chest above his boxer style swim suit made her heart skip a beat, and she swallowed a lump in her throat.

"Well, hello, sleepyhead." He tossed a towel over his head and draped it across his broad muscular shoulders. "Come, join me at the pool."

"I don't swim."

"Just put a suit on and sit in a lounge chair." His coaxing words had a mesmerizing effect on her, and his inviting smile evaporated the small amount of objection she had left.

"Okay, but I'm not getting in the water."

"I'd never force you, Meghan."

She took only a few minutes to change into a one-piece, black swimsuit that Sarah had left at the house. After picking up a towel and her sun glasses, she headed for the pool, where Geoffrey was already swimming laps at a steady, energetic pace.

As she crossed the tiled deck toward a chair, his dark head popped out of the water. "Come stick your feet in. The temperature's perfect."

"I think I'll just sit here."

"Please."

"No."

"Just your feet."

"I'm too scared."

"You don't need to be afraid, I'm right here."

With hesitant movements, she rose and approached the pool. Lowering herself into a seated position on the edge of the shallow end, she closed her eyes and held her breath as the warm liquid encircled her feet and calves. Panic caused her stomach muscles to tighten, and she forced her lungs to fill with air.

She jumped when she felt Geoffrey's hands on her knees. Pressing her lips together, she opened her eyes.

"See, it's not so bad, is it?" His quiet baritone voice sent shivers through her that had nothing to do with her nervousness about the water.

She nodded. "Yes, it is. I hate water."

"How can you hate water, Meghan?" He rubbed her knees with soft, caressing hands. "You have an office on the James River, a house on the Chesapeake Bay, and a vacation home just feet from the Atlantic Ocean. You're surrounded by water everywhere you go."

"It still scares me."

He rubbed his palms along the outside of her thighs and left glistening droplets of water on her skin. "Tell me what makes you so afraid."

"My brother drowned."

"Tell me what happened."

His voice seemed to have the power to coax from her secrets she had long ago promised she would share with no one. His presence made her so comfortable that she wanted to release emotional burdens to him that had always been hers alone.

She took a deep breath. "We were racing in our sea kayaks in the surf, just over the dunes from here. The waves were higher and stronger than usual because of a tropical storm just south of the South Carolina coast. Father warned us not to go out too far, but Jay and I loved the rough waves. He dared me to paddle out as far as I could go. Of course, it was impossible for me to pass up the challenge, but the developing storm made me nervous. The water was more choppy and treacherous than I'd ever experienced. I teased and cajoled Jay into following me away from shore so I wouldn't be out there all alone. As we headed away from shore, we got caught in a rip current that pulled both of us under the surface."

Geoffrey listened with an attentive gaze as he continued

to rub her thighs and knees. She swallowed. "I couldn't pull myself out of it. I thought my lungs would explode as I fought against the force of the current. When I finally managed to raise my head out of the water, I couldn't see Jay. I was frantic as I dove again and again searching for him."

Describing that fateful day brought a rush of painful memories back to her, and tears streamed down her cheeks. Even Geoffrey's caressing hold on her legs provided little comfort at that moment.

"Go on. Tell me what happened next."

A sob caught in her throat. "The local Search and Rescue team worked until after dark, but they found no sign of him. Time crawled by for me in a fog of disbelief and dread. Two days later, Jay's body was discovered by a man surf fishing on a nearby beach."

Through tearful eyes, she gazed at him. "My father told me not to cry. He said I should have been the one to die. Jay was the stronger swimmer, the older one, the only son. He was the one with the promising future; but because of me, my brother was dead. He cleaned out Jay's room and threw away all of his personal things. My father tore up every picture he could find of my brother and then told me that it was my responsibility to take Jay's place as the next president of Blake Industries." She closed her eyes to the sadness and pain that remembering evoked. "I believed my father hated me then. I had lured Jay into the rough ocean waters and killed him."

"Oh, Meghan. It was a terrible accident. You could have died, too." He smoothed her hair away from her tear stained face. "I'm sure that in your father's grief, he didn't realize what he was saying. He couldn't have meant to convince a frightened child of eleven that she was responsible for the act of nature that took his son's life."

"My father was a very imposing man."

"I'm beginning to understand that." He massaged her

shoulders with his hands. "But how does a successful, intelligent woman like yourself continue to be influenced by him? Your father's dead, Meghan. The power he had to make you think you were to blame for your brother's death no longer exists."

She dropped her shoulders and sighed. "In my mind, I know that; but just the fact that my father believed I was responsible for the accident creates enormous amounts of guilt that I still have trouble dismissing, especially at times when I'm having doubts of my own worth."

He embraced her again. "Oh, Meghan, how can such negativity invade your thoughts? You have indescribable worth to your family, to your business, to your friends." He held her to him, and she felt some of her sorrow and fear ebb away.

She leaned against his bronze shoulder. "It must be a family trait."

"What's that?"

"The skill to give magnificent hugs. Sarah says Zach is very proficient at providing comfort with his arms too. I never realized that an embrace could feel so good."

She heard him pull in a sharp breath. "You feel wonderful to me, too, Meghan."

He released her. "I think you need a little swim. Come in with me." His quiet voice urged her as his hands gently squeezed hers.

"Oh, no."

"It'll be okay."

"No, it won't."

"I'll keep you safe, Meghan."

"I can't."

"I'll hold you. You have my word. Trust me." He slid his hands down to her waist. "Your feet will reach the bottom here. It's not very deep."

"It's still water."

"It's just water. Don't be afraid. I'll help you."

She looked into intense gray eyes. "Why?"

"Because I want to help. Because I care. Because you matter, in spite of what your father said." He brushed his lips against her forehead. "Slide in. I have you."

She held her breath as his hands encircled her waist and urged her down into the warm water. With slow, easy movements, he pulled her across the width of the pool.

He chuckled. "You can breathe now, Meghan. Nothing bad will happen to you. I promise."

She gulped air and filled her lungs. "I did it, didn't I?" She grinned. "Well, we did it."

In her excitement, she felt as though she were losing her balance and panicked. Without thinking, she threw her arms around his neck and wrapped her legs around his waist.

If her sudden weight against him surprised him, he didn't show it as his strong arms supported her in a steady hold. "It's all right, Meghan. I won't let you go."

I want to trust you, Geoff. The words were silent in her mind. *I want to be able to accept without condition your presence and your kindness. I want to trust that what I feel for you is love.*

Love? Where had that thought come from?

Her nerves tingled with awareness of him as she clung to his taut muscular body and held on with a mixture of sheer wonder and astonishment. She laid her head on his shoulder and breathed in his familiar masculine scent that so often caused her to feel lightheaded. She nuzzled her nose against the tanned skin of his neck before brushing her lips along his cheek. Her heart stopped as she heard him take a quick breath. Would he respond in the same way her body was responding to his?

With slow gentle movements and without releasing his secure hold on her, he lowered his head until his lips touched hers. For a moment, she worried that he would go no further, simply holding her with his lips as he held the rest of her body with his arms; but then, to her delight, he began to brush first one corner of her mouth and then the other with tender caresses.

Too soon, he lifted his head and sighed. "Oh, Meghan, you do things to me that no woman has ever done."

The spell was broken then, and she shivered. A romantic relationship with Geoffrey would never work. She shivered as disappointment washed over her.

"You're cold. You'd better go dry off."

He lifted her onto the side of the pool. She rushed into the house without looking back at him. Her lips still tingled from the touch of Geoffrey's mouth caressing and teasing them. What was it about this quiet, unassuming man from Boston that caused such emotional turmoil in her?

Their worlds were so far apart. Her life was Blake Industries in Virginia. Geoffrey liked Boston and relaxing at his beach house on Cape Cod. His family was more important to him than anything else in his life. Geoffrey Wright was the kind of man who wanted a family, probably a half a dozen children or so. He was the kind of man who would be a model father as a Little League coach and proud spectator at school sports events, ballet performances and piano recitals. Meghan, on the other hand, was not sure she could ever be a good mother. She thought of the mess she had made of Sarah's life.

No, she and Geoffrey Wright had absolutely nothing in common, and it was pointless to perpetuate the silly notion of developing a permanent relationship with him. As she removed Sarah's swimsuit and stepped into the steamy spray of the shower, her fingers rose instinctively to her lips where the touch of his mouth still lingered.

She wished he did not have the mysterious power to make

her feel so completely safe and comfortable in his arms. She wished her emotions were not constantly aroused by his kind acts and gentle manner.

In silence, Geoffrey tore up lettuce and chopped vegetables to prepare a salad that he thought he would, likely, eat alone. He had scared Meghan. Again and again, he berated himself for giving in to his overwhelming physical attraction for her, and taking advantage of a situation in which he was completely aware of her vulnerability and emotional insecurities.

She had just revealed to him the circumstances of her brother's death and her father's unjust reaction to the tragedy. He had finally convinced her that she would be safe if she entered the pool, that the water was not a threat to her. Why had he pushed her? Why had he chosen to ruin the progress she was making by taking that moment to express the love he had for her? He should have simply enjoyed the fact that Meghan had jumped a huge hurdle and entered the water after years of being afraid of it, but she had been so close to him. She had felt so good in his arms.

He should not have kissed her. Now, he was afraid, he had scared her away, perhaps forever.

He threw pieces of ripe tomato into the salad bowl and chided himself once again. The ringing of the telephone clipped to his waistband startled him. Shaking his head at the instability of his nerves, he fumbled to answer it.

"Hi, Geoff. How are things down there?" Sarah's cheerful voice made him smile, in spite of his dark mood. "I'll bet it's wonderful at the ocean. It's so hot here that we're thinking of moving right into the cove for a few days. Someday I'm going to convince Meghan to install air conditioning in this big old house. Is she well enough to talk?"

"Yes, she's nearly recovered. We even argued about her working this morning."

"See? I told you she'd be a real pain in the neck as soon as she started to feel better. Put her on so I can yell at her."

"She may be napping."

"No, I'm not."

At the sound of Meghan's voice, he looked up to see her standing in the doorway between the kitchen and dining room. He thought his heart would stop at the simple sight of her in blue jeans and faded Harvard T-shirt.

He held the telephone out to her. "It's Sarah."

As she slipped onto a nearby stool and put the receiver to her ear, Geoffrey turned back to the salad. She did not appear terribly upset, although, as he had learned from the past, she was an expert at hiding her true feelings. Her conversation with her sister was brief. When she was finished, she turned off the telephone and set it on the counter.

"Sarah and Zach are driving down from Oregon Inlet, just north of the island, tomorrow afternoon. Sarah wants to take Zach out for some deep sea fishing in Father's boat, *Blake's Bounty,* in the morning. They can hit Gulf Stream waters about fifty miles out and hook into a number of different species."

He chuckled. "Let's hope they have better luck than they did in the cove. Shall we barbecue some steaks when they get here?"

"That sounds good, but I'm not very hungry now after that huge picnic lunch, Geoff, so don't bother cooking. Some salad will be enough for me."

After they ate, she excused herself and retired to her bedroom. Geoffrey spent a few hours reading before he, too, ascended the stairs to his own room. As he passed Meghan's door, he noticed that it was opened; and from it, he heard her voice.

"Jay! Jay! Where are you?" Her words were filled with panic. "I can't find you. Oh, no, no! Sarah, go back. I'll find Jay!"

Geoffrey hurried to the bed and grasped her shoulder. "Wake up, Meghan. You're dreaming."

"No, I have to find them." She shook her head. "Jay, Sarah, where are you?" She screamed and then broke into sobs.

He gave her shoulders a gentle shake. "Meghan, you're dreaming. Wake up, darling."

Her curly lashes fluttered. She stared at him with wide eyes. "What? Geoff? Where am I?" She blinked and swallowed a sob. "I couldn't find Jay, and then Sarah was there in the water with me." Her voice was a breathless whisper. "She slipped under the surface just as I reached for her."

Meghan's body convulsed into uncontrollable sobs. As his chest tightened, Geoffrey drew her into his arms. "I'm here, Meghan. You're safe. Sarah's fine. You were having a nightmare."

She cried against his chest until he thought she could not possibly have any tears left. He thought she cried then for her brother and for her grandmother. She cried all of the tears she had never shed for all of the people she had lost in her life. As her sobs began to subside, she lay her head against his shoulder.

"I'm so cold."

He pulled the blankets up around her, but she continued to shake. "I'll go turn down the air conditioning."

"No, stay with me. Hold me." She wrapped her arms around his waist and took a deep breath. "The water was everywhere. I saw Jay. I reached for him, but he slipped away. Then Sarah was there calling for me to help, but I couldn't reach her either."

Tears flowed again and he held her, wrapped in a bundle of blankets, and tried to give her some small amount of comfort. "It was a dream, Meghan. It's not real." He rocked her with slow, gentle movements. "You're safe and warm here. I'll take care of you."

"I'm supposed to be strong and take care of myself."

"I know, but let me help."

"Why?"

"Because I love you, Meghan."

Chapter Twelve

He held his breath. Had he gone too far? Had he said too much and alarmed her fears again? Would she send him away and out of her life?

"I'm scared, Geoff."

He nuzzled his head in her soft, silky hair. "I know. Nightmares can seem very real sometimes."

"Not the nightmare. Love. Commitment. I'm afraid I wouldn't be able to give you what you need. I work a lot."

He chuckled. "You're right. You do. I admire your dedication."

"I have thousands of employees counting on me."

"And they need you well and alert and creative, as always." She closed her eyes. "I'm so tired right now."

"Then lie down so I can cover you."

"Hold me till I fall asleep?"

"I'll hold you as long as you need me."

With his arms around her, she soon fell into a deep, restful slumber. Lying next to her on the bed and listening to her steady breathing, he knew that, at last, peaceful sleep had come to her.

172

For hours, he lay awake in the dark, unable to sleep. His mind raced with thoughts of weddings and happy endings; but with silent words, he cautioned himself not to rush the issue of marriage with Meghan. She had just grown accustomed to the idea of Sarah and Zach's upcoming wedding. Now she was reliving her brother's tragic death. She had never said she loved him.

It was nearly dawn when he eased himself from her bed and walked in silence to his own room. Leaving the door open in case she called out to him, he undressed and fell into bed, still restless but exhausted, and did not wake until late the next morning.

Meghan did not stir until almost noon, and even then she chose to stay in her room. Barely leaving her bed except to shower and dress, she slept most of the remainder of the day.

Forcing irrational concern for her from his thoughts, he checked on her often and offered her food at meal times, although she seemed to have lost her healthy appetite. Was such a relapse normal? He hoped he was not somehow responsible for it.

When evening came, he began to worry that Sarah and Zach had still not arrived. His concern increased when he could not reach Sarah on her cellular telephone. He was not even sure how far out in the ocean waters a phone signal could be transmitted. As he stared out through the sliding glass doors at the approaching darkness, he hoped that they were just running later than they expected.

"Sarah and Zach should be here by now."

The sound of Meghan's quiet voice tore him from his thoughts. He turned around and saw her crossing the floor toward him.

"Have you heard from them?"

"No."

"They haven't called?"

"Not yet."

"Have you tried calling them?"

"Several times."

"They should be here, Geoff." He could hear the restrained worry in her unsteady voice. "It's after eight. Where could they be?"

"Maybe something held them up."

"What?" She slipped her hand into his.

Meeting her troubled eyes, he forced a smile. "Let's not start worrying yet."

"But I am worried. What could have happened to them? I shouldn't have let them take *Blake's Bounty* out on their own."

He watched her try to control the tears ready to spill from her big brown eyes. He wanted to comfort her but did not know how. He was worried too. "I'm sure they're just running late." He urged her toward the nearby couch.

She chewed her lip. "I shouldn't be here. Sarah wouldn't be coming down if I had been at home. I shouldn't have gotten sick."

The rising panic in her voice troubled him. He slid his arm around her tense shoulders. "You didn't get sick on purpose, Meghan, and Sarah goes where she wants to go. It's not your fault that she's late. You're just upset right now, and you're being irrational."

She gave her head a firm shake. "Sickness is a weakness, Geoff. That's what Father always said. I should have been able to prevent this."

He turned her chin until he could see the consuming terror in her eyes. "Now, that's just ridiculous, Meghan. You must stop this persistent self-punishment. Stop walking in John Blake's footsteps."

She blinked several times and swallowed. He worried that she had been through too much emotional stress during the past days.

He rubbed her shoulders with slow massaging movements. "You are an individual, Meghan, a success in your own right. Your father may have guided you and trained you and helped you perfect your skills, but he's gone now. You're the one who makes the decisions. You are what makes Blake Industries strong and prosperous. You, Meghan, are responsible for its progress."

Her large brown eyes stared at him. Tears trickled down her cheeks.

He cupped her damp face with his palms and took a deep breath. "You can't be John Blake. Stop trying. Just be Meghan. You can be your father's protégé without becoming him. He was an unhappy, lonely man. You will not destroy his memory or his accomplishments by pursuing loving, fulfilling relationships of your own." Lowering his hands to her lap, he gave her trembling fingers a gentle squeeze. "Maybe he never showed it, but I'm sure he would have wanted you to find the happiness he always sought but never found."

She chewed her lip as she considered his words. "Do you really think so?"

Smiling, he nodded. "I think you should have your own office, not your father's with all of his favorite furniture and pieces of art. You spend a lot of hours of your life there. It should be a place where you're comfortable, a place that reflects your interests and what you like. When clients and associates visit, they should see Meghan Blake's personality shining through in the offices and conference rooms, not just John Blake's influence."

She tucked her hair behind her ears. "He wouldn't like me to change things."

"Why not? It's your office now. Add some color and some personal touches. Frame some of your grandmother's seascapes. Display some photographs of you and Sarah. Make it your office."

"I like my father's sculptures."

"Then keep them. Keep what you truly like, but make the office yours."

She grew silent and thoughtful for a moment. Geoffrey breathed a sigh of relief that the panicked expression was easing away from her face.

"Maybe Sarah will help me decorate it. She likes to do that kind of thing."

"I'm sure she would enjoy spending the time with you, Meghan."

Her eyes smiled at him, and she grasped his shoulders. "Has anyone ever told you how wonderful you are? I think I've fallen in love with you, Geoffrey Wright."

His heart somersaulted in his chest. "Is being wonderful better than being despicable?"

"Oh, about that." She grinned. "I may have misspoken yesterday. I was upset—"

"And you had to have a telephone."

She sighed. "You were right, I guess. I wouldn't have rested if I could have worked. You're right a lot. It's a little exasperating, sometimes."

"But you still love me?"

Her brown eyes grew serious. "Lately, every time I promise myself I'm not going to fall apart and cry, you're right there being so nice that I just can't seem to stop myself."

"There's no need for pretense with me, remember. Maybe the reason we met again after all of those years was so that you would have someone's shoulder to cry on when you needed it."

She rolled her eyes. "Destined to be together so I can be an emotional wreck in front of you at regular intervals?"

He smiled. "I wouldn't have put it quite like that, but trusting others doesn't come easy to you. You've admitted that. I believe that you need someone in your life with whom you can feel safe to be yourself."

"So I can be plain old Meghan Blake?"

"Not old and definitely not plain."

"If you're here to provide me with emotional support and unconditional love, then what do I possibly have to give you in return?"

"The same. You share with me your sadness and fear and stubbornness. You let me love those parts of you that you are uncomfortable sharing with anyone else." He kissed her forehead. "I think that's what true love is, darling. It's being yourself with the one person in the world who accepts you for who you really are."

He drew her into his arms and reveled in the declaration of her love. He never wanted to let her go.

The loud unexpected chime of the front doorbell startled them both.

"Sarah and Zach! They must have forgotten their keys."

Hurrying behind her, Geoffrey hoped that she was right, and that Sarah and Zach would be standing on the front porch when Meghan opened the door. He was not prepared for the sight of the uniformed policeman waiting there.

"Miss Blake? I'm Officer Tibbetts of the Dare County Police Department."

"Officer."

Hearing her whispered voice full of fear, Geoffrey moved to slip his arm around her waist. He held his breath.

"We've been trying to reach you. Your phone is out of order, it seems."

"What's wrong, Officer?"

The policeman turned at Geoffrey. "Miss Blake's sister and her companion sent a distress call out to the Coast Guard Station at Oregon Inlet a few hours ago. They were having some engine trouble."

Geoffrey felt Meghan slump toward him, and he tightened his hold to support her. "Are they okay?"

"There's a team out rescuing them right now. We have their coordinates. Are you Geoffrey Wright, sir?"

"Yes, why?"

"Miss Blake's sister gave the dispatcher your cellular phone number so you could be notified of her delay, but I'm afraid we've been having some transmitting problems. The dispatcher couldn't make out the number. The young woman was very concerned about worrying the two of you, so I drove out here to give you the message."

"We certainly appreciate that, Officer Tibbetts. You're sure they're okay?"

He nodded. "A little nervous, probably, and extremely anxious about upsetting Miss Blake." He turned to Meghan. "I understand you've been sick?"

She smiled. "I'm better now, thank you. Geoff, I want to go to the Coast Guard Station. I want to be there when Sarah and Zach are brought in."

"That's really not necessary, Miss Blake—"

"I need to be there. Please, Geoff."

Geoffrey reached out to shake the officer's hand, then turned to Meghan. "I'll go get the car."

The sky was bright with twinkling stars as Meghan waited on the dock next to Geoffrey. A steady breeze of sea air blew as the Coast Guard vessel pulled into the marina, towing *Blake's Bounty* behind it. She felt Geoffrey tighten his hold around her waist, and she could not ignore how much she enjoyed and appreciated his closeness.

Straining to catch the first glimpse of Sarah and Zach, Meghan scanned the deck of the boat. Every muscle in her body was taut, and her nerves felt as brittle as glass. She was so grateful for Geoffrey's calm presence.

Please let Sarah and Zach be okay. Let nothing happen to them. She had said the silent words a thousand times since the police officer had delivered the news that the two young people had had to radio the Coast Guard for assistance.

"Meghan!" Sarah appeared to leap onto the dock and into Meghan's arms in a single action. "Oh, Meghan, I'm so sorry. I knew you would be worried and pacing and driving Geoff crazy with your concern."

Her sister laughed and cried as Meghan held her in a close hug. She felt a huge weight rise from her shoulders as she squeezed Sarah and watched Geoffrey embrace his nephew. She smiled at Sarah. "I was about to take a boat out to search for the two of you myself."

Sarah stepped back and grinned. "I believe it. Geoff probably had to hold you back with all of his might." She caught Zach's hand and pulled him toward them. "The stupid engine quit and, unfortunately, Zach and I are terrible mechanics. We tried and tried but couldn't get it started again."

"And to top it all off, we didn't catch a single fish." Zach smiled. "I hope you have something to eat at the beach house. Sarah and I are starving."

After a late dinner of grilled steaks and salad, Geoffrey and Zach offered to clean up the kitchen so Meghan and Sarah could relax together in the living room. Sarah chose to sit on the footstool while Meghan took a seat on the couch.

"I was scared, but Zach kept calm. When it started to get dark, we knew we had to radio for help." Sarah sighed. "Next time, we're taking you with us. I remember how you could always get that engine going if it quit on us."

Meghan shook her head. "It shouldn't keep having problems. Before anyone takes *Blake's Bounty* out again on the open seas, I'm going to have that engine completely overhauled or replaced, if necessary. I never want to have to worry that someone is out stranded in the ocean again."

She looked up and smiled as Geoffrey entered the living room and strode toward her. Handing her a glass of fruit juice, he took a seat beside her on the couch. She could not ignore the way her heart began to race as his leg brushed hers.

"Blake's Bounty is a wonderful old vessel," Zach said as he gave Sarah a glass of juice also.

Her sister nodded. "And once the engine's fixed, Zach and I want to take her up the coast to Cape Cod."

"What?" Meghan and Geoffrey exclaimed in unison as they shared a look of concern.

"Maybe I'll put the boat in dry dock for about fifty years."

Geoffrey winked at her. "Good idea. It appears that tonight's little mishap was not nearly as frightening for these two as it was for us."

"Speaking of boats," Sarah said as she grinned at Meghan, "I have a wonderful idea for expanding the fund raising activities for the Blake Family Foundation. After spending the past week receiving donations and listening to comments of support from so many enthusiastic and caring people, I came up with the concept of a memorial regatta. We could hold it along the James River or Chesapeake Bay or even down here on Hatteras some time around Independence Day to commemorate Grandma's birthday. What do you think?"

Meghan smiled. "I think that's a great idea."

"I've been doing some thinking about the Foundation too."

Meghan turned to look at Geoffrey, who reached out and clasped her hand. "Early July would be a perfect time for me to arrange a trip down here to Hatteras Island for some of the staff of Wright Pharmaceuticals. After the regatta, maybe we could organize some informal gatherings between them and members of the Foundation to discuss common goals regarding Alzheimer's research."

Meghan felt her eyes widen as he gave her hand a gentle squeeze. "Between your staff and the Blake Foundation?"

His gray eyes held her gaze. "And I was thinking that, perhaps, the president of Blake Industries might want to take time out of her busy schedule to outline to both groups her vision of future financial growth for Wright Pharmaceuticals."

"Oh, Geoff." She realized that the lump that had formed in her throat was not caused by any illness. "Really?"

When he nodded, she leaned toward him and kissed his cheek. He grinned at her. "As president of the Wright Company, I have an obligation to keep an open mind when our competitors present new ideas to us, especially such persuasive and reasonable ones as you have suggested to me."

"Well, it sounds like a plan then." Sarah jumped to her feet. "Come on, Zach. I need to get more juice before we start planning for next July's regatta. Oh, this is going to be so much fun!"

Setting her glass on the table next to the couch, Meghan rose to her feet and strolled through the sliding glass door onto the balcony. She leaned against the railing and looked up at the starry sky as she listened to the rush of the nearby surf.

"Lost in your thoughts?" She heard Geoffrey's quiet voice near her ear.

Her heart began to race as she nodded. His hands rested on her hips, and she felt his warm breath on the back of her neck. She sighed, "You'd probably be surprised at them."

"Oh?"

"We care about each other—" She turned and tipped her head to look at him as her words faded into the night air.

"Yes, we do."

"I'm feeling all sorts of emotions right now."

"Good ones, I hope."

She nodded. "Scary, but good."

"Maybe we should do something about them, the emotions, I mean."

She swallowed. "Like what, for instance?"

He raised his eyebrows. "We could get married and be happy together for the rest of our lives."

She watched a smile tug at the corners of his mouth, and her heart quickened. "We could do that, I suppose."

"Nothing would make me happier, Meghan. Are you sure?"

"I couldn't give up my work."

"Of course not."

"I might be able to manage a vacation now and then."

"That would be wonderful."

"I couldn't possibly take off most of the summer like you do."

He nuzzled the tip of her nose with his. "How about the month of August?"

She caught her bottom lip between her teeth. "Two weeks, maybe."

"I'll take them." He drew her into his arms. "I'll love you forever, Meghan."

"Hey, what's going on out here?"

Meghan peered around Geoffrey's broad shoulder to see Sarah and Zach approaching them, and smiled. "There's going to be a wedding."

"We already know that, silly. In September. Have you forgotten already?"

Meghan shook her head. "No, I mean another one. Geoffrey and I are—"

Sarah squealed and rushed toward them before Meghan could finish her sentence. "Oh, Zach, did you hear? They're getting married. That's wonderful! We should have a double wedding."

"Oh, wouldn't Grandma just love that." Zach grinned and patted his uncle on the back. "Watching both her son and her grandson each marry the woman of his dreams on the same day. What a great idea!"

Chuckling, Geoffrey released Meghan as Sarah pulled her sister into her arms. "Come on, Meghan. What do you say?"

"I don't know, Sarah. Maybe Geoffrey—" She looked up at him, and he shrugged his shoulders.

"Whatever you want, darling."

"It'll be wonderful," Sarah said. "Just wait and see."

Meghan sighed. "September sounds so close."

"Zach and I will do all of the work and make all of the arrangements, won't we?" She grabbed Zach's hand. "Come on. We'd better get started right away."

In the moonlight, Geoffrey gazed down at her. "If things are happening too fast, Meghan, we can wait."

Shaking her head, she moved into his arms. "No, September will be perfect. I love you so much, Geoffrey Wright. I can't believe how happy I am."

He held her as she enjoyed the warmth of his arms around her. She wanted to be his wife. She knew that now. From that moment onward, Geoffrey would be there by her side to give her courage and strength with his unconditional love.